A PURSE TO DIE FOR

Melodie Campbell & Cynthia St-Pierre

A PURSE TO DIE FOR

Copyright © 2012 by Melodie Campbell and Cynthia St-Pierre. All Rights Reserved.

No part of this publication may be reproduced, stored in a retrieval system, or transmitted, in any form or by any means, electronic, mechanical, photocopying, recording, or otherwise, without prior written permission from the authors.

This is a work of fiction. Names, characters, places and incidents either are the product of the authors' imaginations or are used fictitiously. And any resemblance to actual persons, living, dead (or in any other form), business establishments, events, or locales is entirely coincidental.

www.fashionationwithmystery.com

FIRST EDITION trade paperback

Imajin Books

July 30, 2012

ISBN: 978-1-926997-72-8

Cover designed by Ryan Doan, www.ryandoan.com

Praise for A PURSE TO DIE FOR

"Page-turning pace, fascinating characters, sly wit, and a plot that will keep you guessing."—Janet Bolin, Agatha-nominated author of *Dire Threads*

"Fast-paced suspense, charismatic characters, and dialogue to die for. Brisk plotting with a deadly twist at the end."—Lou Allin, author of *She Felt No Pain*

"Campbell and St-Pierre have style in the way they present, develop and portray their characters. This novel grabs hold of you from the get go with its cast of wacky and malicious relations. A delightful novel with complex relationships and a series of shocking secrets. The authors have a knack for wonderful turns of phrase, which are one reason why this novel is a delight to read. Then there is one mystery after another and suspense building to an unforgettable conclusion. Campbell and St-Pierre create a delectable concoction of savoury and unsavoury characters, sex, delicious humour and suspense. This winning combination can't help but delight readers."—Garry Ryan, Lambda-nominated author of *Malabarista*

"An old-fashioned murder with modern sensibility; stylish characterization, and delicious plot; artistically woven."—Rebekkah Adams, author of *Front Porch Mannequins*

Cynthia's Dedication:

To Yves, for giving me the means to write, as well as the motive, and to Melodie for the opportunity.

Melodie's Dedication:

Dedicated to Mom, the original fashionista, who walked the Rainbow Runway just before this book was published. Miss you every day.

~*~

Cynthia's Acknowledgements:

Love to Becki, writer extraordinaire, for encouraging, inspiring, and being my sister. Thanks Gail, Sheila, Cathy and Karen for hanging with me all these years, and still you're my gang. Paul, you're the nicest collision reconstruction officer I know, and I promised, like, decades ago I'd thank you in a book. Finally, to the rest of my dear family and friends, in order for me to thank you all as you deserve, here's hoping for plenty of follow-up books!

Melodie's Acknowledgements:

Melodie wishes to thank *Vogue* magazine, a fixture in the parental home for over 60 years, plus her parents, who dressed her like a fashion princess from the age of one.

Chapter 1

Gina ran. Each pounding step took her further away from the death of her grandmother, the house full of relatives and thoughts of Tony.

Running in the early morning gave her a sense of peace and power that fuelled her entire day. Working under television cameras was insanely stressful. She cherished the relief that came with solitary running.

She moved at a moderate pace, taking in the vibrant foliage and clean air. This was not the time to think. This was cleansing time. She jogged along Centre Street into town with a plan to re-approach the house from the forest at the back.

The trees sparkled with morning sun bouncing off leaves. Gina kept to the path and slowed her pace to a walk as she entered the clearing that led to her grandmother's property. Someone was sitting on the bench by the back fence.

She moved forward and then smiled. "Aunt Mandy! Tony will be pleased. When did you get in?"

Aunt Mandy's eyes were wide and fearful. She opened her mouth, but nothing came out.

"What's wrong?" Gina noticed Tony standing just a little ways off and there was something at his feet. A pile of something red.

"Gina, don't come any closer," he warned. His voice was like gravel.

She moved as if something pulled her forward. She took in the gold purse, the red dress on the twisted female body and farther off, the baseball bat streaked with blood.

"Gina," Tony pleaded.

Far away, she could hear her own voice screaming.

Chapter 2

Four days earlier…

Gina brought her hand up to shield her brown eyes from the sun. The park was a splendour of deep green, red and gold, signalling the last few weeks of autumn. In the clearing, a dark-haired man wearing jeans and a tan golf shirt sat on the ground with his back against a maple tree. His good-looking face split into a grin as she approached.

"Hi, Squirt," Tony said.

"Hi, yourself," she said, grinning back. Nobody else called her "Squirt." "Somehow I knew you'd be here." She swung herself to the ground beside him. The leaves of autumn cushioned the hard earth beneath the tree.

"Waiting for you, Cuz. Damn, but it's good to see you."

She reached for his hand and squeezed. That's as far as she would ever go. They weren't kissing cousins. That would be too dangerous, for her heart, anyway. He would always treat her like a beloved kid sister, of course. *Of all the rotten luck, to have a crush on a relative.*

She looked into Tony's friendly blue eyes and felt right at home.

"How's my favourite Weather Network babe?" he asked.

She smiled. "Predicting stormy weather back at the ranch."

"That's a sure bet. Been to the house yet?"

"No. I came here to the park first. I figured you'd be at the old maple."

Tony pulled his knees up and folded strong arms around them. "My favourite tree in the whole world—yeah, I've got a special feeling for this old beauty." He seemed perfectly at peace. "We spent every holiday up north here, didn't we? Sometimes I think it was just being around all this wood that inspired me to be an architect."

"There is a rather tree-house effect with most of your designs," she said. "I love the mix of wood and modern and soaring light. When I walk into one of your houses, it does something to my soul."

Tony smiled. "Thank you, Gina. That's high praise indeed."

They sat in companionable silence for a moment. Sparrows flitted across the branches overhead and dappled sunlight made a pretty pattern on the ground.

"Still seeing Claudia?" she asked. She flicked a long strand of chestnut hair over her shoulder.

"Nah, that ended a while ago. She was a little too 'uptown' for me. No doubt you thought the same."

Gina relaxed and for once kept her mouth shut.

"How about you and lawyer-boy?"

"Oh, that's over," she said. "I think he thought more of himself than of me. And I got a bit tired of being shown off all over town like a prize horse."

"That's what comes from looking the way you do, kiddo."

"What, I look like a horse?"

Tony laughed. "Only one with a goddess figure. You know what I mean. Take a compliment when it's offered. Those are killer jeans, by the way. I like the sparkly thing on the back."

Gina smiled. "Rock & Republic."

"Still the fashionista. I guess that's supposed to mean something."

She smiled again and looked down at the ground. Tiny ants marched single-file a short distance from her feet, going about their business, oblivious to the threat only inches away. She would have to remember not to step on them as she stood up. "Do you know how she died?"

"I don't know the details. Aunt Carla seemed...cryptic. Do you mind much?"

She wriggled, uncomfortable. "Grandma was always scolding you and riding Ian. I can't ever remember her telling anyone she loved them."

Tony scowled. "I'm not sure she was capable of love. But if she loved anyone, it was you. We all do."

Gina turned to face him, but he had closed his eyes. "You taught me how to burn leaves here."

"What?"

"With a magnifying glass. Remember? It was about this time of year. You held it over a dead leaf to magnify the sun and it started to sizzle. The leaf, I mean."

Tony laughed. "Oh, that. Yup, I got in big doo-doo that time. Juvenile delinquent corrupting the pretty young cousin. Ian was such a tattle-tale."

"He's done pretty well for himself with that new cable show."

"Who would have guessed that both my cousins would end up television stars? You a meteorologist, and Ian a big-shot interior designer." He reached forward and ruffled her chestnut hair. Then he vaulted to his feet and held out a hand. "Come on, Squirt. Ready to face the dragons?"

"Will he be coming tonight?" Gina asked, rising.

"Ian? You forget the will. If there's money, he'll be here."

Ian stared at his face in the motel mirror and shuddered. He looked all of his thirty-three years. Too much coffee and not enough sleep. Well, what could he expect? The train ride from the city had been harrowing. Too bad he'd never learned to drive a car, but if one lived in a civilized place like Toronto, surely it made more sense to leave the driving to professionals.

He sighed and surveyed the surroundings. Wouldn't the *Design at Nine* production team just about drop dead to see him here? The worn carpet was a nondescript colour. Greige? Andrew would get a good giggle out of that. The shabby sea-foam green draperies and bedspread screamed 1980. *Did we really have such appalling taste in those days? Mother-dear would have a coronary if she could see this.*

Why couldn't they have a decent hotel in this town? He sat on the bed and heard a spring boing.

No way, though. No way was he going to sleep over in that demonic house, even if the parents stayed there. True, the old bitch was gone—that was the only reason for being here—but there would still be Uncle-Pompous-Ass to deal with. Better to stay in this no-class wasteland than have to rub shoulders with that disgusting bigot.

He placed his Louie Vuitton on the bed and opened it. So the old lady was dead. Well, about time. He sniffed, but not in sorrow. He'd always hated going there as a kid, being constantly measured for worth and found wanting. Was the grand-bitch even capable of love? Yes, he got the same as Gina and Tony every Christmas and birthday, fifty dollars in a cheap white envelope, but it was given grudgingly in the name of fairness. Surely there had to be something for him in the will. And if it were enough—dear God, it had to be enough—then he could keep Andrew from straying. Dear Andrew...so lovely to look at and so famous, now that the show had gone international. But money would make all the difference. Andrew was surprisingly addicted to comfort for one so young.

He pulled open a bureau drawer, sniffed it and wondered if it was safe for his Y-fronts.

"Close the window, Jerry. It's wrecking my hair."

Jerry grumbled and reached for the window switch of the old BMW. Now the smoke would stay in the car and within minutes he would be gasping. Why did he let her get away with bossing him around? He glanced over at Linda, beautiful, aging Linda, as she put out a cigarette in the ashtray. He wondered if he would ever be able to walk away, leave her for good.

"Mind the black car, Jer—oh, what a jerk! Did you see that? Some people don't deserve to live. How much longer have we got to go? I need the ladies, and I don't want you stopping at some flea-bit place."

"You didn't have to come in the first place," he mumbled. "What's the point of it? I'm the one mentioned in the will."

"What's the point of it?" Linda turned in her seat. "What's the point? Are you crazy? Did it not occur to you that I need to be there to protect your interests? And Ian's, let me remind you. Even now, I'll bet the vultures are circling, putting their dibs on the best stuff. I'll bet sister-dear has her eye on the Lalique, and I'm damned if one of the kids is going to sneak off with the ruby set. None of your family appreciates good jewellery. None." She flashed a slim hand laden with diamonds.

"Ian can take care of himself," he muttered.

"Ian would want me there and you know it."

Jerry gazed at the road ahead. His thoughts were grim as he imagined the next few days. Relatives bickering over TV sets and antique china. It was sordid, that's what it was.

"And don't give me any grief about caring about the old woman. She was a bitch. Look at the money she gave your brother to set up that business. Did she ever once give you a cent when you needed it? No! Poisonous old biddy. I couldn't stand her and neither could you." Linda snapped open the vanity mirror on the back of the visor and stared at herself.

He grunted but kept his thoughts private. They didn't need a bigger house, anyway. Did anybody really need more than 3,500 square feet? Ian hadn't lived at home for years. What was the point? Mother had been right—just more for Linda, as usual.

He kept his eyes on the road and tried to imagine his life without the woman sitting next to him. Did he love her anymore? He certainly had when they were younger. Jerry couldn't believe his luck thirty-five years ago when he landed such a beauty. Indeed, all the other partners in the chartered accountant firm congratulated him. That magnificent black hair and blue eyes—such a rare combination. It felt good to be envied. To be fair, Linda was a still a looker and could pass for ten years younger. But it had come at a price, of course. A big price.

The CA in Larry kicked in. *That's the trouble with life. Everything comes at a price.*

Chapter 3

Becki faced the luxurious oak casket, topped with an arrangement of roses, lilies and daisies. She had made a huge mistake including her over-cheery favourites. Too casual. Not as offensive as snapdragons, but close.

Eventually Godmom's casket was lowered into its rectangular hole. She had to admit the ritual sickened her as much as it did six-year-old Nellie, who was parting with her lunch off to one side. It never got any easier. So long ago, Mom and then Father had died. As the years flew by, the Grim Reaper had snatched away relatives of friends, then friends of friends, then dear friends themselves, and, dammit, now Godmom. She felt twice as old as Methuselah. Judging by her former teenage standards, she *was* ancient. Younger than Joan Rivers, younger than John Travolta. Yes, but older than Catherine Zeta-Jones. *Still her doppelganger.*

Godmom dead.

She wondered how an accidental smothering worked exactly.

Her husband, Karl, was Chief of Police of Black Currant Bay, so maybe that had something to do with the feeling something was a wee bit off.

Nellie finally fell asleep in her room, which relieved Carla. She was able to appreciate how pleasant it was to spend time with her big brother, Jerry, after all these years, even if he was probably only present for the funeral and the reading of the will. Even if he'd felt it necessary to bring Linda.

Standing in the dining room, which usually felt grandiose, but today felt inadequate, Carla was surrounded by the bustle of the on-going, post-funeral reception, including the ring of serving utensils on china plates and the choruses of *Oh my, I haven't seen you since*...It felt like a miracle to have the opportunity to talk with her favourite brother. Not at all right, she knew, to have a favourite brother. But even Jerry would never dare joke that she only preferred him because Giuseppe was long dead. The solemn occasion, the crowd and the level of noise in the room lent an intimacy to their brother-sister tête-à-tête. If only she could completely shrug off the awkwardness from not having seen each other of late.

"Nellie's grown so much," Jerry said.

"How about your TV-star son? Freaks me out Ian's older than me."

"You watch his show?"

"Course."

Holding back a section of her layered, shoulder-length, dirty-blond hair, she hunched her lean frame slightly to take a bite of the sandwich she'd chosen from the catered buffet. Filling oozed onto the corner of her mouth, and she used a finger to guide the egg salad in. *Hard enough to maintain an image,* she thought, *without having egg on your face.* Luckily Jerry was momentarily distracted by loud laughter from Gina and Tony and didn't seem to notice.

"Mom allowed *Design at Nine* to broadcast in her house?" he asked as soon as he turned back.

"She could hardly stop me from watching what I wanted in the privacy of our room."

"Just can't figure out how you were able to stand living here with her."

"No choice."

"Reggie still doesn't have a job?"

She looked around to make sure Reggie wasn't within hearing distance. "He's working again, but you know about the gambling debts. Then there's child support for Mark. It's taking longer than we thought to build up a down payment. No point wasting our money on some cheap house on the wrong side of town, right? If Mom taught us anything..."

"...it was to buy quality," Jerry finished. "Yup, she taught us that." He glanced at Linda, who was still busy ogling the selection of silver trays set out on the mahogany table.

Nellie was proud of one thing about herself, and that was being the best in the whole wide world at pretending to be asleep.

After Mom tip-toed out and shut the door, she whispered to Macho, monkey king of her stuffed animal kingdom, "I saw that detective guy hanging around the cemetery."

Macho looked concerned.

"Mom said he was there to pay respects, but didn't want to intrude. And you know what else she said? She said that pile of dirt beside Grandma's coffin was so men could fill in the hole over Grandma after we left. Gross, right?"

Macho nodded.

She cried. And after a while, she said, "I'm going to take a peek at what's going on downstairs. Want to come?"

Chapter 4

It was hot in the dining room. Gina rushed in a little late and discreetly slid into the single unoccupied antique chair at the far side of the huge oval table. She mouthed "hi" at Becki beside her, who smiled back. Sun poured in from the bay window behind her. The large green dining room, normally so cold, seemed stifling today.

Across the table and down toward the head of it, she could see Tony and Ian, listening intently. The lawyer, a well-fed man with glasses and receding grey hair, sat in the one remaining dining-room chair with arms. The back of his head reflected in the mirror that served as the back wall of Grandma's enormous china cabinet. The contents within the hutch were a young girl's treasure trove. Many times as a child, Gina had stared at the colourful Depression glass, the painted china tea cups and the figurines, wishing she could take them out and...

Oh, dear. The lawyer paused in his talk and was looking at her. He frowned. Gina felt herself blush. The man then cleared his throat, continued reading.

"'To my dear goddaughter, Rebekkah, I leave my Piaget diamond watch to remember me by and two hundred thousand dollars with which to travel the world. We spent many a pleasant hour dreaming about places to visit. Now I want you to do it.'"

Becki made a choking-sob sound. Gina smiled inwardly with satisfaction. It was so good that Grandma had thought to give Becki these things. Gina nearly reached for her hand and then stopped herself, realizing it might cause Becki to react even more emotionally. Instead, she fixed her eyes on the painting that graced the opposite wall. Definitely an old-world hunting scene with mounted riders and dogs. As a kid that picture had both haunted and fascinated her. She'd always been glad the fox was offstage.

The lawyer looked up once more.

"I have been left strict instructions to read the next bit verbatim:

'I am a proud woman, one who values dignity. I admit to some disappointment regarding my own offspring. I expect even now they are sparring over china and silver, items of paltry value that can make no difference to their standard of living. I have seen other families ripped apart by human vultures fighting over remains of little value. It disgusts me, but I fear it to be probable among my own children and their spouses, and I won't have it. For this reason, I have elected to leave the bulk of my estate to the next generation.'"

There was a collective gasp.

"What the hell—" Jerry yelled from down the table.

The lawyer ignored this and continued. "'To my dear granddaughter, Nellie, I leave you this house and all the contents, with the exception of the aforementioned items. These will be left in trust and deeded to you upon your 18th birthday. I leave you an additional one million dollars in trust, which you will also receive on your 18th birthday. It is my express wish you will use this for your education and for maintenance of this house, which I hope you will continue to inhabit. I trust this will allow your parents to live in the manner to which they have become accustomed.'"

Gina giggled—she couldn't help herself.

The lawyer grunted and looked up fiercely. "'To my remaining three adult grandchildren, Ian, Tony and Gina, I leave the remainder of my estate to be divided equally.'" The lawyer paused. "She leaves a note concerning each of you, which she has requested I read aloud. 'Ian, I expect you will squander your entire inheritance on decadent living. I trust you will have the decency to practice any sordid behaviour discreetly.'"

Ian's gasp was audible.

The lawyer continued. "'Tony, although you are not of my blood, I feel you are the grandchild most like me in many ways, and thus I include you as an equal legatee. Practice your architectural design talent well and make our name proud.'"

Gina felt the shocked silence around the room. What did it mean? She looked at Tony, who seemed equally puzzled. He leaned forward.

"What does she mean, 'not of my blood'?"

The lawyer took off his glasses. "You're adopted. Surely you knew."

"No," Tony said. "I didn't know." He looked absolutely stunned.

"Well, that explains the blue eyes," Jerry said.

"What on earth do you mean?" Linda asked, fumbling with a compact.

"No one has had blue eyes in this family for three generations. And Mandy has brown eyes too. So it's scientifically improbable. Blue eyes are recessive."

Linda snapped the compact shut and turned to scold him. "If you knew that all these years, why didn't you say something?"

Jerry shrugged. "I always figured Mandy had an affair."

Tony was out of his chair in an instant. "Why, you—"

Ian grabbed him by the arm. "Hold on there, mate. Keep it cool."

Gina rose to her feet. "But...but that means you're not my cousin."

There was stunned silence in the room. Gina glanced around, stricken. This had come out all wrong. Aunt Linda looked horrified. Ian's mouth was open and Tony—well, Tony was staring straight at her.

"I mean," Gina blurted, "of course you're my cousin, you'll always be my cousin, but we're not..." She couldn't find the word. The room grew even hotter.

Tony looked odd. "No, I guess we're not."

Gina sat down with a plop. Her face burned.

"Young lady, children who are legally adopted have all the rights of natural children in this country," the lawyer said sternly. "Tony has as much right to this inheritance as you do."

"Oh, no!" Gina cried. "I didn't mean—" She stopped, aghast.

"What she means is," Tony leapt to the rescue, "we're all a bit shocked about this unexpected turn of events and need some time to take it in. But by all means, go on with the reading."

The lawyer reached for his glasses and cleared his throat. "To my beloved granddaughter, Gina, I wish a lifetime of happiness. The security of this inheritance should allow you to marry whom you wish and pursue your career dreams."

"See? I was right." Tony said softly. "She did love you."

"Sir? Ummm, Mr. Hadley? Have you any idea how much a third of the remainder will be?" Ian's voice was high and strident.

The lawyer stared at Ian with disapproving eyes. "After the initial gifts and endowments are taken care of and probate paid...I would imagine...in the neighbourhood of two million. I can't be exact, of course."

"Two million—" Ian shot to his feet.

Linda was stunned. "Two million? That means she had over seven million dollars. Jerry, where did she get all that money? And why didn't you know about it?"

"I can't believe she didn't leave me anything." Jerry slammed shut the door to the guest room.

Linda's laugh was verging on hysterical. "It's the final insult, isn't it? The old bitch had to have the last laugh, as always."

"It's a disgrace—that's what it is—that I have to go to my own son for money. I'll never forgive her. Never."

Linda gazed critically into the en-suite mirror. "At least Ian is a sweetie. He'll share nicely, you wait and see."

Jerry sat on the edge of the bed. "It's the principle of the thing. I can understand her not wanting Reggie to have it. He's such a loser. But I'm a successful businessman. Why did she doubt me?"

Linda shrugged into the mirror. "She's a harridan. One of those ghastly hags from the old myths. What would you expect?"

"Or maybe..." Jerry brightened, "maybe she thought I was so successful, I wouldn't need the money and would be insulted by it? Do you think that could be it?"

Linda nearly choked. "Hardly. She was hateful and you know it. She meant it to hurt."

Jerry fell back onto the bed. "The whole thing was a waste," he mumbled. "Why did I bother?"

Linda turned from the mirror. "What was a waste? Jerry, what are you talking about?" Her voice was sharp.

Gina stood on the terrace waiting for Tony to join her. With the lawyer gone, everyone had awkwardly scattered. Uncle Jerry was the first to go, storming out with Aunt Linda creating a perfumed wake. Reggie and Carla disappeared somewhere. Tony had accompanied the lawyer to the door.

What was she to make of it all? On one hand, there was the surprise of becoming suddenly rich. How thrillingly wonderful it would be not worrying about money anymore. At the same time, she felt a twinge of guilt. What about her parents? Would they resent being overlooked in favour of the next generation, in the way that Ian's parents obviously felt? She closed her eyes. It was absolutely imperative there not be a rift in her own family over this. Right then and there she pledged to put half the inheritance in her parents' names. They could enjoy an even better retirement.

"Deep in thought?" Tony had crept up behind her.

Gina kept her eyes focused on the garden. A few late roses bravely withstood the change in season. "It is a lot to think about. You, more than anyone."

He frowned. "Can't say I'm looking forward to the confrontation. It won't be pleasant. I wonder why she didn't tell me."

She looked down at her feet. "I expect there was a very good reason. I can think of at least one."

"Give," Tony said.

Gina sighed and wondered how much she should say. But she had never been able to hide her thoughts from Tony.

"Your parents were out in Vancouver for three years. The family never saw your mom pregnant, which I guess is why no one questioned anything." *Except Grandma, who knew everything about everyone.* "Have you thought maybe the adoption wasn't completely legit? Perhaps they didn't go through all the correct channels, like a waitlist. It was the late 70s, after all. It wouldn't have been hard to find a girl willing to give up her baby with no fuss."

"Mom was never very patient," Tony mumbled.

"In any case, it doesn't matter. Adoptions don't affect anything once you're over the age of eighteen," she said. "And then, when you were over eighteen, why rock the boat? I can imagine she saw it was best for everyone. You're named by name in the will, so you inherit regardless. It really doesn't matter."

"Doesn't it?" he said enigmatically. "I think it matters rather a lot."

Gina stepped back toward the sliding glass door. "You're thinking the health implications of not knowing who your birth parents are? Yes, I can imagine that would matter to you."

"I wasn't thinking of that," Tony answered.

"You can't touch the capital, Reggie. It's in trust. The lawyer made it quite clear." Carla busied herself making the bed so she wouldn't have to look at him.

"You must have said something to make her do this. Treat us like a bunch of kids. What the heck did you do?" Reggie stormed around the room.

"I didn't do anything," Carla grumbled, firmly tucking in a corner. *I just married you.*

"Becki, can I talk to you for a minute? Come out here to the garden, if you don't mind." Tony gestured from the back porch. Although he preferred modern architecture, he appreciated the graciousness of Grandma's red-brick Georgian Revival...its classical proportions, hipped roof, columns, pilasters, cornices and spacious porches.

Becki joined him and they stepped down in silence to the back garden. The large maple tree there was starting to turn scarlet. Langdon Hills was blessed with hundreds of towering maples just like it on private properties all over town and in the town park up the street. Squirrels scampered across the yard on personal missions.

"Something's bothering me and I want to bounce it off you," Tony said.

"Is it about Gina?"

"No, actually." He looked quizzical. "How...? Although I probably will want to talk to you about all that at some other time." He kicked a stone onto the garden edge. "I was thinking about the way Grandmother died. Has anybody said anything? The police? Does it seem strange to you?"

Becki was silent for a moment. Then she said, "I've been wondering what to do about this. Yes, it does seem odd. I was going to talk to Karl because I just don't know enough about how people die this way. He might be able to get his hands on the autopsy results. I wouldn't have said anything about it at all because why kill an old lady for the sake of a rickety old house? But the money is unexpected. It changes things. Do you know how she came to have so much money, Tony?"

"Actually, I do." Tony frowned. "The thing is...who else knew she had that kind of money? You didn't know. And I'm sure Gina didn't, either. Did any of the others?"

"I've no idea," said Becki. "But it makes for a heck of a motive."

"Gina, I need to talk to you."

Tony's voice reached her from behind as she mounted the stairs. "I'm just going up—"

"Now, Gina. It's important."

She turned around to face him. He looked so earnest, just like a boy. Always, he had the power to persuade her. Gina sighed and descended the stairs.

"Let's go outside," he said.

They walked out the front door. "Come off the porch." He leaped down. "I don't want anyone overhearing."

Gina followed him warily. Not now—she didn't want to talk about the whole library scene. She didn't feel clever enough to cover up her true feelings.

"I want you to leave the house and go home today," Tony said. He looked ready to burst.

Gina nearly fell over. What was this? She said nothing.

"It's too dangerous here. You might get hurt. You need to go home so I know you're safe." He blurted it.

"What are you talking about?"

Tony paced around her like a herding dog. "I think Grandma was murdered. I think someone knew how much money she had and put a pillow over her head."

Her mouth flew open. "You're crazy."

"Becki thinks it's possible too. I've just talked with her. I want you out of here." Tony stopped and stared into her eyes.

Gina was caught in a whirlpool. *Grandma murdered? One of the family? Who? Why?*

Tony seemed to read her mind. "The killer may not have known what was in the will, that the money skipped a generation. You know what they say about it being easy to kill a second time if you can get away with it once. They may target one of the heirs now to make the pot bigger."

She felt her mind spinning. If she wasn't safe, neither was Tony. Or Ian or Nellie, for that matter. *Could anyone be so heartless as to hurt Nellie?* That settled it. Finally, she said, "The Queen Mum."

"What are you talking about?"

"What she said during World War II. 'The children won't go without me, I won't go without the King, and the King will never leave.'"

Tony looked puzzled. Then his eyes seemed to click into focus. "You won't go unless I do."

"That's right. And we can't leave Nellie."

"I'm not going, Gina. I can't."

"I figured that." She crossed her arms over her chest.

"I don't like it," he said, frowning.

"That's tough," Gina replied.

Chapter 5

"I'm sure they'll enjoy any hot breakfast, after yesterday."

"Who're you talking to?" a small voice asked.

Becki twirled and discovered Nellie staring at her. "Who am I talking to?" she repeated, stalling for time, hand on heart. "Good question. Um…"

She could tell Nellie she was talking to herself, but she didn't approve of lying to children. To anybody. Even little white lies.

"I was talking to Mom, who isn't really here in person, because unfortunately she happens to be…uh…dead. Normally I keep conversations with Mom private, but these old floors," she squeaked a board with her toe, "forgot to creak and warn me I wasn't alone. And you caught me."

"Dead like Grandma?" asked Nellie, pie-eyed. A little ragamuffin.

"Right." With vigour, she continued to whisk the bowl of eggs, vanilla and salt.

"That's okay, Aunt Becki, I talk to Macho."

She smiled in relief. "And Macho is…?"

"My monkey. He's up in my room right now. Father doesn't like it if I bring Macho down and walk around the house with him. He says I'm not a baby anymore. And of course I'm not."

"Of course you're not. You're a lovely little girl."

"If he knew I talked with Macho, he'd be so mad. Nobody else knows but me and Macho. And now you."

Feeling touched by the non-judgementalism of children and privileged her niece shared her secret about Macho, Becki said, "Well, if you keep my secret, I'll keep yours."

"Deal." Nellie held out her little hand. "Shake."

Becki took Nellie's delicate hand in hers and solemnly shook it, wishing the skin over her own knuckles didn't look and feel quite so tree-barkish in comparison.

"What're you making?" Nellie asked.

"Breakfast. You like French toast?"

Nellie nodded, staring at the counter and all the culinary activity evidenced there.

"Want to help?"

"Yes."

"Would you like to set the table?"

Nellie hesitated.

"It's an important job. We'll need knives and forks." Becki dug into the utensil drawer and counted out the right number. Making her way toward the table, she said, "I'll leave them all here. Put one fork and one knife in front of each chair. I'm sure you know forks go on the left and knives on the right. Oh, and napkins." She searched the buffet along the far wall. "Which colour do you like best? Plain red or bright yellow with pictures of roosters and hens?"

"Both."

"Good idea. Let's put a red one at one setting, then a yellow one at the next. You going be a designer when you grow up?"

"You're a designer right?"

"I'm a designer. You going to be a politician when you grow up?"

"Why?"

"You answer questions with questions."

Carla and Reggie entered the kitchen. Carla, thin, fair and pleasant-looking. Reggie, thick, dark and scowling. Carla must see him as muscular, seductive and aloof. Big mistake as far as Becki was concerned.

"Morning," she said. "You're a bit early. Haven't quite finished. But help yourselves to juice. It's on the table."

"Since we had Nellie," Carla said, pulling out a chair, "we never get to sleep in. Though sometimes I let Reggie catch a few extra Zs. Smells like you're treating us to something yummy."

"Thought we could all use a little cheer."

"Should be a ban on cheer in the morning," Reggie said. He squinted in the light.

Becki dipped both sides of another piece of bread into the egg mixture. She laid it on the greased griddle with a sizzle. The aroma of butter and vanilla drifted up. When it was ready, she said, "Help yourselves from the bowl of strawberries and the pitcher of maple syrup on the table."

The others walked in.

"Making French toast," Becki said. "Yours is up shortly."

"How cool is that," Gina said. "What can I help you with?"

"Bring the food to the table when it's ready?"

"Perfect."

"You're a short order cook too, Aunt Becki?" Tony asked when Gina handed him his plate.

"Know my way around a kitchen."

"Write a food column for a paper, don't you?" Jerry said.

She was surprised he remembered. *"How to Spot an Aspiring Vegetarian."*

"That's why there isn't any bacon," said Reggie.

"But not complaining. Delicious. Thank you," Tony said.

"You're very welcome. Is Ian coming?"

"He was."

Becki decided to grab a plate for herself and join the others at the table.

"Have any of you made plans since the big reveal?" Linda's raven hair, which was pulled back in a ponytail, gleamed like the lacquer on her nails.

Jerry nudged her. "Money's not a subject for the table."

"How many times have you dragged me to a restaurant for dinner with people I don't even know, and all we talked about all night long was money?"

"That was business."

"I'm just saying, it's interesting," Linda continued. "I mean, some of us need money more than others. You, for instance, Reggie. But the old broad sure fooled you, didn't she?"

Stunned silence. Except Reggie, who stood so quickly his chair fell backward, hitting the floor with a splintering sound. His teeth were clenched as tightly as his fists.

Ian chose that moment to saunter into the room.

In an effort to relieve the tension, he said in his pitchy voice, "Mother, Mother, off the wall..."

"Can I give you a hand?" Gina grabbed a dishtowel from the pantry closet.

"Sure. Thanks." Becki smiled. Her hands were busy with a soapy pan. "Most of the dishes are in the dishwasher. I'm just doing the leftover bowls and pans. Somehow I'm not surprised to see you here."

Gina grabbed a pan from the drying tray. "Just like old times. You here on holidays, and me following you around like a little puppy."

Becki laughed. "True, how true. Those were really nice times. I loved coming here, being part of a real family. But I was thinking more that it would be you who volunteered to help with the work. Should you be doing it in that outfit? It's gorgeous on you, by the way."

"Thanks," Gina said. "I know this designer discount place—I really should take you there."

Becki just smiled.

"Besides, who else is there? Carla is trying to get Nellie to do her homework—always a daunting task. And Linda? Seriously, can you picture Linda offering to do housework?"

Becki frowned. "I think she and Jerry were meeting with the lawyer about something or other."

"Poor fellow." Gina grinned. She could just imagine the scene—Linda trying to charm the lawyer into seeing their side of the picture, and Jerry attempting to bully the man with the threat of a lawsuit to challenge the will.

"Do you honestly think they could overturn the will?" she asked.

"No." Becki was thoughtful. "I can't imagine anyone suggesting your grandmother didn't have all her senses when that will was signed. No one could support that. She knew what she was doing."

Gina sighed and picked up a large bowl from the tray. "They aren't going to like it. And I feel funny about my parents. I can understand her not wanting Linda and Reggie to get hold of her money, but why would she cut out my mom?"

Becki pulled the plug from the sink, letting the water drain. "I think it was a matter of fairness. This way it seems fair. Each arm of the family gets the same amount of money. It just goes to the next generation. They get control. And she knew you would share with your mom. You'd give a stray dog your very last bread crust, Gina."

"I like dogs," muttered Gina. "Not sure about all my relatives."

"Mom?" Gina yelled into the cellphone. "Oh, Mom! I'm so glad to hear your voice."

"Me too, sweetie. Has it been too awful?"

"Pretty ghastly, Mom. Linda and Jerry are seeing a lawyer. And Reggie looks like he's going to hit somebody. Becki's here keeping everything going, thank goodness."

"Good for Becki. Give her a hug for me. We'll be home by the fourteenth to help out with everything."

Gina felt herself relax. "Has it been a nice cruise?"

"Wonderful. Your dad is actually sleeping well and we both need to go on diets. And the shopping. Lots to tell, but mainly I'm concerned about you. Now don't you go feeling guilty a bit about this will. I knew about it and agreed with Mother this was the best thing to do. I just didn't expect to be away to leave you facing it alone. Sorry, Pumpkin."

"I'm not alone. Tony's here, thankfully. Oh my goodness, did you hear about Tony being adopted, Mom?"

"Yes, sweetie, I've known for years. Mandy told me. But don't tell Tony that."

"I'm so embarrassed. I was such a fool in the library. I made everyone think it made such a difference. And it doesn't at all."

"Doesn't it?" The voice through the cell seemed to be fading. "I would imagine it makes rather a lot of difference."

Chapter 6

Carla crept out of the bathroom adjoining their bedroom. She'd dried her tears and changed. A long-sleeved sweat shirt. Sweat pants. Clothes that hung loosely against her torso. Soft, comfortable clothes. And no one would see the bruises. As she walked toward the bed, she said, "Maybe I should tell everyone Mom was sick."

He was sitting on the bed. Feet over the edge. "She didn't want you to, right?" There was still an edge to his voice.

"No." She sat down beside him. She knew what would settle him down. When he locked his arm around her waist, she only winced a little.

Canadian weather is so weird. Then Becki remembered her last trip to the Dominican and realized it's exactly the same all over the world. One minute sunny and you think it's safe to go for a picnic or invite friends over for a BBQ, and the next minute it dumps on you.

Not a great afternoon for setting off on a long drive. Should she go? Should she stay? Since Carla told her privately about Godmom's cancer, and how it was advanced enough she took sleeping pills over and above pain medication every night before going to sleep, she'd decided to call Karl.

"See, on the one hand, cancer explains everything," she told him, "but on the other, the news doesn't settle my mind."

"Why not?"

"Did someone snuff out Godmom's life, thinking he or she was saving her from terrible end days? Or did Godmom request someone help her with an assisted suicide?"

"Anything's possible, but the coroner labelled your godmom's fatality a death by natural causes. If he had evidence showing human intervention, he never would have released the body for burial."

"Right."

"So you're coming home?"

In her mind she saw Karl's lips curve in a smile.

"What evidence would indicate death by unnatural causes?" she blurted.

"In your human intervention scenario? Signs of struggle. Bruising on the face caused by something pressed over nose and mouth."

"Apparently Godmom took sleeping pills to knock herself out every night."

"So accidental smothering is within the realm of possibility. She was found on her stomach, right? Maybe she was too weak to lift her head up and away from the bedding. You know, like crib death. Your godmother was old and frail. But think about it. Precisely because she was old and sick, maybe she just stopped breathing. When it's my turn, honey, that's how I'd prefer the Grim Reaper take me. In my sleep."

"I suppose."

"One last point to ease your mind," Karl said. "Say it was murder or euthanasia or whatever. Why would your godmom's killer leave the weapon there on her head?"

"You think it just landed there?"

"Maybe her body jerked involuntarily. Tipped a pillow from the head of the bed."

They discussed possibilities until Becki said, "Thanks for all your input, hon. I appreciate it. I guess we can talk about it more when I get home."

A half-hour later, Becki peered out the window as the rain continued to smear itself across the window pane. Water gushed along the gutters of the street below. Trees on the boulevard flailed in the wind.

Someone rapped on her door.

Opening it, she was surprised to find Gina and Tony in the hall.

"Can we talk to you, Aunt Becki?" Tony asked.

"Course. Come in."

"You're leaving?" Gina asked, referring to the suitcase on the bed.

"Well, I came for Godmom's birthday, ended up staying for her funeral and the reading of the will, and Karl is waiting for me at home."

"What about what we talked about earlier?" Tony asked. "In the garden?"

"I ran into Carla even before I talked to Karl. Did you know your grandma was sick?"

"No."

Becki shared Carla's information and described her telephone conversation. Outside, the rain continued to pound, and though it was afternoon, it felt like early evening.

Tony reached for Gina's hand then and suddenly changed his mind. "Just had this bad feeling in my gut."

"You're not going in this weather, Becki," Gina cut in.

Becki shrugged. "Won't last for ever."

"Maybe we should all stay one more night," Tony suggested.

Chapter 7

"Have you seen my Blackberry?" Jerry charged into the guestroom in a fury.

"You left it in the car," Linda said, turning from the closet. "Just what are you so het up about all of a sudden?"

"That money," he grumbled. "How can I be her executor and not even know about it? Nearly eight million dollars! I swear it wasn't there when Dad died. So where did it come from?"

Linda shrugged. "Maybe she got left it by another relative. Maybe she had an affair with a wealthy lover."

Jerry looked wild.

"No, that's not very likely," Linda conceded. "I know. Maybe she won a lottery."

He gave her a black look. "I'll tell you, someone had to know. And I'll bet that someone killed her."

"Oh, Jerry, don't be foolish." She lifted an empty hanger. "What does it matter? The old bitch is dead, thank the Lord. Don't go thrashing around stirring things up now."

"I'll thrash around as much as I want," he muttered. "She was my mother, dammit. I'm going to make some calls outside in the car…get on the track of her broker. He should know something and I'll make him tell me. I am the executor, after all."

"You do that," she said quietly. She waited a full two minutes after he left before starting down the stairs.

Cancer. Just the thought of it made Gina shiver. Had they been wrong, then? Was Grandma's death natural, or—Gina had to face the thought—did Grandma plan her own ending? Somehow, Gina couldn't imagine the grand old lady submitting to the indignity of illness and its treatment. Perhaps, after all, her death had been a good thing. In any case, she could talk with the others about it later at dinner.

Gina headed slowly down the stairs in search of late afternoon coffee. No hope of a Starbucks within fifty miles, so it had to be the kitchen.

"What do you mean you don't do house calls up here?" Linda's strident phone voice carried along the corridor. "I know there's a storm, but how am I supposed to know the difference between sterling and plate? This stuff looks eighteenth century, so that would make it sterling, right? Check for the mark on the bottom...what mark? I haven't my glasses here, for crissake. Hold on a sec."

Linda spotted Gina, covered the mouthpiece, and said, "What are you still doing here?"

Gina stopped abruptly. "Tony and I have to be at the lawyer's office on Monday, so we're staying the weekend." She stopped short of asking what Linda was still doing here.

"Do you know anything about silver?" Linda hissed.

"Not a thing," said Gina, shaking her head.

Linda sounded exasperated. "It's important. I only get one choice from the lot, so I can't make a mistake."

"I thought Jerry got to choose something," Gina said, feigning innocence.

Linda snorted. "Jerry doesn't know the cost of anything."

And Linda knew the value of nothing. *What a pair,* Gina thought. She smiled as she carried on down the hallway.

Nellie was in the kitchen, sitting at the old wooden table with that old monkey of hers for company.

"Hi, Pumpkin," Gina said cheerfully. "Is that hot chocolate you're drinking? I may have some too. Quicker than coffee. You know we're staying the weekend?"

Nellie grinned. "Mom told me. That's super-duper. We're playing Rumoli tomorrow and I'm going to beat the pants off Tony."

"Good." Gina smiled. "I'll play too."

"We're playing with pennies," she warned.

Gina filled the kettle with water. "Glad you warned me. I'll have to keep on my toes."

She sat down, waiting for the kettle to boil. She took the time to look carefully at Nellie. Her brown hair was uncombed and she was wearing a stained orange t-shirt with ratty old jeans. It occurred to Gina that—in the maelstrom of the last two days—no one had been taking very much time with Nellie.

"How are you doing, sweetheart? This must be pretty devastating. I know you cared a lot about her. And goodness knows, this kitchen doesn't seem the same without her in it."

Nellie frowned. "I loved Grandma. I don't know why everybody else didn't. She was great. She let us live here for free, even."

Gina looked down at her hands and tried to find the right words. "I think they were afraid of her. Even I was a little afraid. How can I explain it? She seemed to know everyone's weakness and made a point of letting them know she knew."

"What's so bad about that?" Nellie grumbled. "I wouldn't be scared about that. That's silly."

Gina laughed. "People are silly when it comes to their pride, Nellie. Very silly. But you're not. You remind me of her a great deal, you know, but only in good ways."

Nellie looked up. "What ways?"

Gina paused. She looked around the faded kitchen, taking in the solid wooden cupboards, the genuine tile floor, and the heirloom table. Everything solid and comfortable, and no-nonsense...not apologizing for itself, not pretending to be something it wasn't.

"You're smart. She was quick as a whip. You're a survivor, just like she was. And you look like her. You're going to be very pretty when you're older. She was, you know."

Nellie grinned. "I know. I've seen some old photos. They're funny."

Gina nodded. "I wouldn't want to wear those clothes from the forties. Girdles—yick."

"What's a girdle?" asked Nellie.

"Look it up on the net." Gina rose from the table. The kettle started a mournful whistle. She reached for a mug in the cupboard. "You have one other quality that she didn't have, sweetie."

"What's that?"

"You're kind," said Gina thoughtfully. "And in the long run, that's the most important quality of all."

Ian stared at the cellphone in his hand as if willing it to talk. Why wasn't Andrew answering? Where could he be? He felt the panic rise in his throat. And here he was with all this good news to share. *Two million dollars. Who would have thought?*

Ian threw the cellphone down on the bed. He paced to the window and looked past the parking lot to the dark green hills beyond. Rain had stopped momentarily, but the wind was whipping through fields and bending trees. He hated the country. *Gawd, the bugs. Give me a room on the 34th floor of a Marriott in any major city and a chocolate on the pillow at night...blessed civilization.*

He checked his watch. They were meeting back at the house for dinner, which meant, in this weather, he should leave soon. At some point he would get Tony and Gina aside, and pump them for details.

What was there between Gina and Tony, anyway? Something was up. Ian was pretty savvy about these things and he sure had a sense of kissing cousins. Well, that was okay by him. And no messy genetic crap now, if they decided to have babies.

Wonder who Tony's real parents are? He never did look Italian enough for this family.

The cellphone rang and he leapt for it. "Yes? Oh, hi, Mom. I'll be there for dinner. No, you don't have to come and get me. I can walk. It's not that bad."

He listened for a moment.

"No, I didn't know," he said. "How awful."

"Fine, we'll talk tonight. Love you too." He turned off the phone and sat down on the bed.

Cancer. Who would have thought it? The old girl always seemed too tough for any disease to take hold and survive in her rawhide body.

Ian shivered. He knew about disease. Two friends had lived with HIV, fighting it for years only to waste away to nothing. It was horrible. Just like cancer.

Whoa! There was a brainwave. Maybe she did herself in. Grandma would never accept losing her dignity. His thoughts were a maelstrom. *Oh gawd, would that affect the will? What does suicide do to a will? Or does it just affect insurance? And where the heck did all that money come from, anyway? Surely someone in the family would know.*

Ian gazed out the window and frowned. Then he was up on his feet in a flash. His gaze followed a man and a woman dashing across the parking lot to a car. The car was unknown to him, but the woman was vaguely familiar. Good looking too, in a soggy Kim Novak way.

Now *that* was interesting.

The man glanced over his shoulder once before disappearing from view.

Holy Cats Cannoli, what's going on here?

A sly smile spread across Ian's face. For if there was one code he lived by, it was this: knowledge is power.

Chapter 8

It was 6:00, cocktail time.

"So I want to set the record straight," Carla said.

She looked around the room, staring them all in the eyes, one by one. Thanks to those singing lessons—the ones she begged for when she was a child not much older than Nellie—she'd learned how to hold the attention of an audience while performing.

"Mom's passing is not as surprising or as sudden as you may have been thinking to yourselves," she said. "Mom didn't want me to tell you, but..."

She paused to give her words effect, even if she suspected by telling Becki earlier, without asking her to keep it to herself, most of the room was already up to speed.

"...she had cancer." She raised her glass. "Here's to Mom. May she rest in peace."

The room was quiet. What was wrong with everyone? They looked embarrassed. Becki was staring down at the table. Even Gina wouldn't meet her eyes. So they already knew, just as she suspected.

Jerry cleared his throat. "Why didn't you tell me before, Carla? And why didn't *she*?"

Carla went immediately on defense. "You know what she was like, Jerry. Never show a weakness. She only told me a week ago."

"What kind of cancer?" This, from Linda. "Was it contagious?"

There was a gasp and a chair scuffled against the floor.

"I don't know." Carla heard her voice become strident. "She didn't tell me. Some kind of internal thing. I don't know. She wasn't feeling well. That was why she had to say something. It couldn't have been that far along in that she didn't look very sick. All I know is she didn't intend to wait it out. No chemo and radiation for her, no sir." Carla threw her glass of wine back and took a large swallow. She put the glass down and frowned. "Don't blame her. Lose your hair and your looks? Better to die," she said grimly.

"She should have told me," Jerry grumbled.

"Who the hell cares?" Reggie said. "She's dead now. That's what counts."

Carla turned her head away. *Shut up, Reg. Jesus Christ, shut up.*

"Now, what exactly do you mean by that?" Tony's voice was smooth.

"Not a thing." Reg shot him a glare. "But dead is dead. Hardly matters how you get there."

Mundane chatter after this.

Jerry wondered where Mom's larger-than-expected fortune might have come from. Linda wanted to know if Mom kept anything of particular value hidden away for safety's sake. Nellie, Tony and Gina talked about a Rumoli game taking place tomorrow and would she like to join in? Ian huddled with Reggie by the desk, and when she looked their way, Reggie sent her one of his charming smiles. The old expression, "he could charm the pants off you," fitted him well.

Becki was quoting Albert Einstein. "'Nothing will benefit human health or increase the chances for survival of life on earth as the evolution to a vegetarian diet—'"

"If you'll excuse me," Carla interrupted. "I'm just going to pop into the washroom before we go in to supper."

Phew! She shut the door of the main-floor powder room and plopped down on the upholstered chair facing the pedestal sink. She grabbed a copy of *Chatelaine* from the side table and idly read the subscription information.

FIORENZA FERRERO
123 HAWTHORN AVENUE
LANGDON HILLS, ONTARIO

She studied her reflection in the gilt mirror above the basin. She didn't inherit Fiorenza's dark eyes, dark hair or olive skin. But at least she, Carla Williamson, didn't tout tofu or quote Einstein, like Mom's can-do-no-wrong goddaughter.

She washed her hands, flicked off the light and exited.

On her way back to the library, she heard Reggie talking in the living room. Obviously on the phone. She was just about to enter the room and coax him into coming back with her when she noted his angry tone. She couldn't help but overhear a sentence or two.

"For God's sake!" he hissed. "Someone already saw us once. Fine! Tonight in the alley behind the house."

Supper started at 7:00. Everyone took the same spot around the dining room table as at the kitchen table for breakfast. Like a real family or something. Nellie knew that's what real families did 'cause when she went to her friend's house for sleepovers, Abigail's father always sat at the head of the table and her mother at the other end of the table. Nellie and Abigail squeezed in on one side and Abigail's little brother, who was only four and a real pain in the butt, on the other side. That's how it worked.

But at Abigail's, they talked about cool things like the family's trip to the zoo in Toronto, and what her and Abigail's favourite cartoon was on TV, and what Mr. and Mrs. Spencer watched when they were little. Here, Nellie didn't get a chance to say much of anything, and when she did, they all stared at her like she was the same age as Abigail's little brother.

For example, when she demanded, "What *is* this?" She poked at her food with the tines of her fork.

"It's Tuscan poached tilapia with green beans," Ian said.

"Tuscan?" Nellie asked.

"As in Tuscany. A region of Italy."

"Grandma was from Italy and she didn't make stuff like this."

"Hmmm."

Nobody seemed to want to discuss it. "What's tilapia?" she insisted.

Mom said, "It's fish, honey. Try it. You'll like it."

"Don't eat fish."

"I usually don't, either," Aunt Becki said, "but it's good. You'll see. Tomatoes, olives...I bet even a little white wine."

The wine drew Nellie's interest.

"Your cousin Ian's a man of many talents," continued Aunt Becki.

"Like sticking his nose where it doesn't belong," Father said.

"I called Karl again to explain I wasn't leaving until tomorrow after all," Becki said during dessert. *Why do I always feel responsible for prompting conversation?*

"Was he very upset?" Carla asked.

"Oh, he never gets upset about little things like that."

"Some guys don't get excited about much of anything," Reggie said.

Tony shook his head. "I can imagine certain things get Uncle Karl riled up."

"His work," Becki agreed.

"Totally dig it," Ian said. "Last *Design at Nine* makeover, we had to tear everything out and start from scratch. It was such a disgrace. A straight man hangs a giant flat screen on the wall and thinks he's Ty Pennington."

Reggie snorted. "At least straight guys don't sing *'Oh, I think a pink throw would look marvellous over there by the picture window.'*"

"Just ignore Reggie," Linda said.

Becki did just that. "Glad to hear you're not advising your viewers to run out and buy the latest in electronics, Ian."

"Why're you glad about that?" Linda asked.

"Manufacturers don't need designers' help swamping people with product. Over 91,000 tonnes of electronics are sold every year in Ontario."

"Wow!" Gina said.

"And where do TVs, VCRs and CD players end up when new versions hit the market?" Becki asked.

"Landfill," Gina replied.

"The ugly consumer and all that," Tony said.

"Oh, don't get me wrong," Becki said. "I'm a capitalist. Have my own shop and everything so I'm not immune to the *good life*."

"Yet this afternoon," Linda interrupted, "you were headed home before seeing the lawyer about your Piaget diamond watch and two hundred thousand dollars."

It was night-time again. The worst time. Tonight it was thundering and lightning. She pleaded with Mom to let her leave one light on, but the shadows were still spooky even if Macho told her not to be afraid.

"But, Macho, something could happen here in my room and they'd all be playing cards downstairs or sleeping in their own rooms. They wouldn't notice anything was wrong until next morning when they found me dead in my bed."

Not like Grandma, Macho said.

"*Exactly* like Grandma."

She lay awake and tried to count sheep. The sky grew lighter and lighter as the night wore on. The moon came out from behind the clouds. It was kind of pretty, but all she wanted was for the moon to go to sleep and the sun to come up.

Chapter 9

Gina stood at the bedroom window and gazed out onto the backyard. It seemed to go on for miles and miles in the dark. And that's just the way she felt—in the dark.

A windfall of two million dollars. Grandma dying of cancer. Tony not her cousin. What else hadn't she known? How were you supposed to keep your balance when everything you thought to be true suddenly got turned on its head?

"We've got to talk," Tony had whispered after dinner when they were clearing the plates.

"Not now," she had said. "I need to help Becki and Ian clear up."

"Then meet me at—"

"Tony, can we do this tomorrow?" She felt the panic rise. "It's nearly nine. I'm exhausted. I just want to go to bed."

She could see his eyes turn dark with disappointment. He moved away a bit, and looked so unhappy she almost recanted.

Because it wasn't true. She wasn't tired...only scared of facing the confrontation. That there would be one, she was sure. They would have to talk about this new aspect to their relationship. Could things go on as before? Could she pretend nothing had changed? The barrier of blood that had braced Gina for keeping her feelings in check was now gone. Vanished.

She would face it tomorrow when they met for breakfast. Everything would be clearer in the morning. She turned from the window, just missing the lone figure as it raced across the lawn.

What a hell of a day. Tony didn't feel like going to bed yet. When a truck hits you in the face, you don't feel like sleeping. He went in search of a stiff drink.

Jerry was sitting on the library sofa holding a glass.

"See you had the same idea," he said with a welcome grin.

Tony headed to the drinks trolley, reached for a glass and poured whiskey from a decanter. "The drink of life," he said grimly. "Cheers." He flopped down in an easy chair.

Jerry saluted with his glass. "Linda is doing some sort of facial thing. Can't stand that kind of primping, so I cleared out."

Tony nodded. He wasn't feeling a desire for female company at the moment.

He gazed about the room. What a handsome place. He'd always loved the oak-panelled walls, the big stone fireplace and the comfortable furniture. When Tony was young, he thought there must be a thousand books in here. One rainy day he went about counting them. He counted all day in between meals, stopping only when he reached three thousand. And that wasn't half.

"The thing I can't figure out is where she got the money from." Jerry was raring to talk. "Eight million dollars, for crissake. How come I didn't know about it?"

The old clock struck a quarter chime. Tony drank from the glass and pondered his reply.

"Where the heck did she get it?" Jerry continued to puzzle.

Tony was silent. Then he made his decision. "She inherited it from Italy two years ago. Some great uncle died, leaving her and two other cousins a bunch of apartment buildings in Palermo. They bought her out." So the cat was out of the bag. Let the chips fall where they may.

Jerry rose to his feet. "You knew? She told you?"

Tony nodded.

"How long have you known?"

"From the beginning."

Jerry started to pace like a caged animal. "I can't believe it. Does anyone else know?"

"Just you now. She made me promise."

"Why you and not me?" Jerry insisted. "I'm her son—why didn't she tell me?"

"That's simple," Tony offered. "I'm the only one in the family who speaks proper Italian. Remember, I did that exchange program in Rome for my degree. The papers from Italy were in the Siena dialect, which is what they now call *Italian*. Grandma was born in Palermo. She spoke and read only the Sicilian dialect. She needed someone who could translate and she wanted someone in the family."

He left it at that. No need to point out both Jerry and Reggie would have figured out a way to get at that money. And Grandma damn well knew it.

"Oh. That makes sense." Jerry ran a shaky hand through his hair. "But why didn't she tell me after? Why didn't she trust me?"

Tony sighed. "Jerry, you know how she was. She loved knowing a secret and holding it over everyone. She probably would have told you eventually when she could have used it for something, like preventing you from going away. I don't know."

Jerry plunked down on the sofa. "The crafty old bitch." He finished the glass of whiskey and slammed it down on the end table. "One thing for sure. Wait until good ol' Reg hears about this. Eight million dollars right under his very nose all this time and he doesn't even know it's there." He started to laugh and when the tears started to fall down his face, Tony joined in.

Chapter 10

Carla woke rather suddenly. It was morning. She didn't know how she dared, but she poked Reggie several times to wake him. He dragged himself into a half-sitting position and pulled the covers up over his torso. She noted his rheumy eyes and his slackened limbs. He never woke up alert the way she did.

"Woke up in the middle of the night and you were gone," she said.

"Huh? Give me a break. What time is it?"

"Heard you talking on the phone before supper yesterday. You agreed to meet someone in the alley last night. That where you were, Reggie?"

"None of your business."

"You all paid up now? 'Cause I've decided I'm not gonna deal with your gambling anymore. Not your gambling. Not your fists. None of it!" She glared at him.

"What's got into you?"

"You snuck out again. After you promised."

"Well, where were *you*?" he demanded. "When I got back, *you* were gone.

"Had to pee," she said. "Then I checked on our daughter. That's where I was. And you're in no position to point fingers. Don't even know why I let you sleep, when I came back and saw you lying there snoring."

"Admit it, baby, you love me," he said, his voice like butter.

His skin was warm when he touched her. No, hot. He kissed her lips. She smelled his masculine scent. Damn, but he could always make her believe. "Maybe there's hope…" she said, pulling away, "…and only because Mom left Nellie a fortune…and we can make a good life…like we planned long ago. Make Nellie happy. Travel all over the world if we want to. But not if you ruin it, Reggie."

His bedroom eyes examined her.

"I'll divorce you," she threatened. "I'll get custody of our daughter and you'll be out in the cold, Reggie. I mean it!"

"What you talking about, woman?"

"I deserve better than I've been getting," she said, traitor tears accumulating. "I so deserve better."

"Can't get better than me, baby," he said—confident, seductive Reggie.

"Oh my Lord! What's going on now?" Becki wondered. Out her bedroom window she saw three police cars lined up along the curb in front of the house.

Must be a hostage situation.

"Mom, be reasonable."

Maybe Nellie's been kidnapped.

"God forbid!"

A drunk and disorderly?

"Don't you *know* what's happening, Mom?"

Since when have I ever been able to tip you off about something before you found out for yourself?

"Makes me think being dead doesn't have that many advantages."

You're telling me!

Becki dressed hastily. She wasn't a robe kind of person. Especially not when staying at someone else's house. She pulled on a clean pair of black jeans, which obviously shrunk last time she washed them. A black t-shirt, which seemed snug too. Made sense. Vegetarians are prone to excessive carb consumption. Next, she combed her dark hair into a pony tail. She found if she kept it tight enough, there was a slight lifting effect to the face. She unrolled a pair of socks and slipped them on. Washing her face and applying all the various creams that were necessary when you were fifty would have to wait until she reassured herself everything was fine. The police cars were only parked in front of 123 Hawthorne because…

Down the stairs. No one in the library. No one in the living room. No one in the dining room.

She poked her head into every room, including Godmom's quarters, just in case, but the ground floor was empty. False alarm. Plenty of time to go back upstairs, even have a bath before breakfast, then her long trip home. She glanced out a back window to assess the kind of day it was going to be after the unsettled weather last night.

She spotted a police car in the alley behind the garage. Not to mention a blue-uniformed cop. She left the house by the back door. Crunching maple leaves underfoot, she waved to Gina. Gina was wearing a lovely, form-fitting jogging outfit. Becki didn't think it was tight because it somehow shrunk in the wash. Usually friendly, Gina didn't wave back. Instead, she bent over like she had stitches in her side. Or needed to redirect blood to her head so she wouldn't pass out. Or was about to hurl.

Tony dashed to Gina's side. Then he looked up at Becki and made an awkward, jerky movement. Not an effective salutation. Somehow, the whole scene whispered *sinister*. However, not being a just-ignore-what-you-don't-want-to-know kind of woman, Becki continued on. Cops barked ominous commands. A woman sitting on a bench turned.

"Mandy!" Becki exclaimed. She bent down and hugged this dear woman—was surprised to find her cheek cold and moist. "Been such a long time! So nice to see you!"

"And you." But Fiorenza's daughter-in-law, Tony's mother, directed her eyes toward yellow plastic tape, wrapped carelessly around trees and other less natural markers.

And Becki saw what the fuss was all about. Inside the barrier was a body.

Most people just ignore six-year-olds. But the detective Nellie saw at Grandma's funeral had set up in the library and he was interviewing everybody. Including her. Mom walked into the room with her. Held her hand.

Nellie peered up at the detective. He was sitting behind the desk. The lamp she and Mom liked was turned on and all sorts of pretty colours reflected off the top of the desk. They were told to sit in the chairs in front of him, like he was the teacher and they were the students.

"Nellie, I'm Detective Dumont. How're you?"

"Fine."

"Did your mom tell you what happened?"

"Yes."

"Will you answer some questions for me?"

"Okay."

He got up, pushed his chair back and walked down one side of the room. She didn't follow him with her eyes. Didn't want to.

"Did you notice anything different about last night?" he asked, his voice coming now from the back of the room.

"Last night it was thundering and lightning out," she said.

Mom nodded, smiled at her and squeezed her hand as if saying, *'You're doing fine.'*

"Anything else?"

"Couldn't sleep."

"Why couldn't you sleep?" he asked, his voice floating across from the other side of the room.

"Scared."

"Of what?"

"Lightning." *Duh.*

"Did you hear anything out of the ordinary?"

"Where?"

"Anywhere."

"The grown-ups downstairs. We had company."

"What were the grown-ups doing?"

"Eating, drinking, talking and stuff."

"Did anyone come up and see you?"

"Not after Mom tucked me in."

Detective Dumont slumped back into his chair. "If I show you a picture of a woman, would you be able to tell me if you've seen her before?"

"Guess so."

He passed a picture to Mom, who examined it carefully, like when she looked through books Nellie picked out at the library before they checked them out. She passed the picture to Nellie.

Because Mom had said some strange lady was found at the end of their property, Nellie expected it to be a picture of someone she didn't know. Someone she'd never seen. But when she glanced at the picture, she jumped in her seat and a noise flew out from the back of her throat. She suddenly didn't want to hold the photo. Her hand wobbled when she handed the picture back to Detective Dumont.

"Recognize her?"

She remembered the night when she woke up and waited for Mom to come in and check on her. The bedroom door had creaked open and light from the hall shone on the heavy curtains covering her window and the foot of her bed where her animals were lined up, and the blank wall beside her bed where Mom's silhouette projected like a shadow puppet growing larger as she approached the bed. Not turning her head—because she was supposed to be asleep—Nellie had opened her eyes just a bit and found some *other* woman leaning over her.

"Ahhh!"

Nellie thought she'd better not say the other woman looked as surprised in the photo as when Nellie yelled, *"I want Mom!"*

But the detective prodded, "You have something you want to say?"

She shook her head.

"Tell me," he said, his voice rising.

Mom frowned at him. Mom never let anyone, not even Father, raise his voice at her.

"Can I ask a question?" Nellie wondered.

"Of course."

She pointed. "That's a picture of the lady you found outside?"

"Yes."

In a voice that sounded wavery, even to her, she asked, "She's dead?"

Chapter 11

The room grew thick with tension. Nellie pretended to concentrate. She frowned for effect. "I think she came to the house once. I saw her ring the doorbell, but nobody else was home, so I didn't answer."

"How long ago was this?" the big man asked.

Nellie shrugged. "Maybe two weeks ago?"

"Hon, you never told me," Carla scolded.

"Wasn't nothing to tell. You told me to never answer the door. So I didn't."

"What time of day was this?"

"Right after school." The fibbing was getting easier. "You were with Grandma at the stores. I don't know where Father was."

"Was she carrying anything?" the detective asked.

"Can't remember. I only saw her from the upstairs window." She tried to act disinterested.

"What day of the week was this, Nellie?"

"Can't remember."

"If it was two weeks ago, that must have been Thursday," Carla said. "I took Mom to the dentist. We were away longer than usual."

"Was it Thursday, Nellie?"

"Maybe. Don't know." Nellie looked down at the floor. "Can I go now?"

"Rob Dumont. Who would believe it?" Tony said as he sat with

Gina in the kitchen, waiting to be interviewed.

"Is that a good thing?" She had a good reason for asking.

"It should be. I've known him for years, although I haven't seen him in about five. He's smart and level-headed, which is a blessing in a cop. Don't you remember playing Beckon with him and the other local kids in the summer?"

Gina nodded. Those early days were wonderful times. The older boys taking control like they were minor gods. Everyone playing together outside until the streetlights came on.

Tony smiled. His eyes had a dreamy look, as if they were sifting back through long-ago visions.

"He was about a year older than me. So, yeah, you would have been a little squirt at the time. He was a big, good-natured kid and I hung with him for years. He taught me how to smoke behind the garage." Tony smiled at the memory.

They sat quietly for a moment.

"I remember when he got accepted into the force," Tony said. "I was here for spring break and we had one hell of a whoop-up at the Tap Room in town. I had to get three guys to help me carry him home."

"I remember him. I think he used to like me a little." Gina twisted a napkin around her fingers.

"You're kidding!"

Gina looked away. "You weren't always here when I was."

Tony frowned. "He didn't try anything, did he?"

"He never asked me out, per se. But sometimes when I was fourteen or fifteen, he would show up with wildflowers and take me for walks." *Silly thing to say. I sound like a dog, being taken for walks.*

"Bloody hell. Good thing I didn't know. I would have knocked his block off."

"He was rather sweet about it." *Until he wasn't.*

"Well, he never told me." Tony sounded like he'd been betrayed. "He was too damn scared to tell me."

Or maybe just careful, Gina concluded. Darned if she could ever comprehend why males acted the way they did. Surely, if she had dated a friend of Tony's, it would be a good thing.

The clock ticked. Gina forced herself to the present. She hated what was next to come. Soon they would all be interviewed individually and she'd have to go in without Tony.

She shivered. "You say he's smart. Will he be kind?"

"He'll be fair. He'll want evidence and he won't jump to conclusions. And that's what we need now."

A tall, lanky policeman came to the doorway and signalled for

Tony.

"Back in a few minutes," he said. Then suddenly, as if compelled—as if taking a giant step toward something unknown—he reached down and kissed her. Then he was gone.

Gina sat, nursing her coffee. She felt as if the air had been sucked out of the room. Everything was moving forward, and she was being sucked along in the wake, helpless.

She remembered Rob Dumont. She remembered him very well, indeed. And she certainly hadn't told Tony everything.

"Tony. Long time, no see." Rob Dumont reached forward to shake hands, hoping his old friend wasn't involved. Tony's grasp was firm.

"Sorry it took something like this to get us together, Dumont. And congratulations on the promotion." Tony sat down.

"Thanks." Dumont's eyebrow lifted in appraisal. "You still work out, I see."

Tony laughed. "Remember those comic book ads we used to mull over? How to become a He-man—Atlas, something?"

Dumont grinned. "Yeah, I remember. Never worked for me, but I guess you have to keep at it." He was quiet for a minute. "Tony, what do you know about this?"

"Not much. Gina—you remember Gina, of course?"

Dumont nodded. He would never forget Gina. That was his curse. The years seemed to melt away as he visualized a pretty young girl with brown curls and hazel-green eyes. His heart heaved a bit.

"Gina was out for a run," Tony continued, "and I went out to wait for her in the garden. I got as far as the woods and found my mother sitting on a bench in shock. You've seen the site. The body was on the ground about ten feet away. Didn't look like it'd been moved."

Dumont frowned. *To trust, or not?* He made up his mind. "It wasn't."

"Body was cold, Dumont. Rigor was over far as I could tell. I checked that to be sure. Didn't want to disturb the scene."

"This isn't anything to do with you, is it, Tony?"

Tony's head snapped up. "No."

Dumont stared at him. "Are you still working for—?"

Tony leaned forward. "I'm an architect. You know that. It allows me to do a lot of travel."

So that's how things were. Dumont had expected as much. "Gotcha. So, it's not about anything you're doing now."

Tony shook his head. "Never seen the woman before. She wasn't carrying. And the fact she was killed by a whack on the head…"

"You mean if it had been a gunshot or a ligature—"

"Yeah. Not premeditated." Tony leaned back in the chair.

Therefore, not an assassin. That's what Tony was trying to tell him. And that was good. It meant the case was still his, instead of the Fed's.

"So...why on your property, do you think?"

Tony shrugged. "I don't know if it's connected to the family or not, but there's something you might want to look into."

Dumont sat up.

"You know we're all here for the funeral. My grandmother's death was a bit of a shock. She had recently inherited eight million dollars. And yes, I knew about it. I'm not entirely satisfied she went as the doctor claims. I suggest you check into it."

Dumont scratched his chin. "You think she was—"

"Before you ask, I don't know what this woman had to do with the family, if anything. But we've always been straight with each other before. I'll help you as much as I can. That goes without saying."

"That means you don't suspect your mother or Gina." Dumont smiled.

"Mom has arthritis. You'll find that out soon. She can hardly walk with a cane, let alone wield a bat. And Gina..." Tony's voice softened, though there was an edge to it. A threat.

Dumont rose from behind the desk. "I understand. There's a murderer loose. You're here to protect her. We'll do our best."

Tony gave a curt nod. "Come get me after you interview the others. I think it's best you get your own picture first. Then we can talk. I'll be around."

The interview was over for now.

Tony stood up and held out his hand again. Dumont took it.

As Tony headed toward the door, Dumont said, "You carrying?"

Tony turned slowly and smiled. "Always."

Chapter 12

"It's *my* job to decide the order of witnesses," Detective Dumont replied.

"Just saying…weren't Tony, Mandy, Gina and Becki the ones on the scene?"

"My job to ask the questions." He frowned, but the tic at the corner of his mouth told Carla he was holding back a more pleasant expression. "Plus, I did talk to your nephew."

"When?"

"After my interview with Nellie," he said. "You were probably getting her set up with some new activity."

She didn't change her outward posture, but on the inside, she let herself relax a little. It's not like the detective thought she was the one who bashed the other woman's brains in. And if her daughter could handle being interrogated, for heaven's sake, she could too. Besides, she knew Detective Dumont way back when he was just "Rob," a neighbourhood kid. It was he who had recently handled Mother's death. Now, as then, he didn't appear nearly as badass as Reggie.

"You saw the picture of the victim," Dumont said. "Do you know her? Have you seen her before?"

"Never."

"Your daughter said she came to the house."

"When we were gone."

"And the reason for her visit?"

"How should I know?"

"Humour me."

"Avon calling?"

Dumont smiled in spite of himself. "Any more brainwaves?"

"Isn't coming up with brainwaves *your* job, like deciding the order of witnesses and asking the questions?"

Detective Dumont cleared his throat. "She shows up at your front door one day. Dies practically on your back lawn on another. Explain that."

"Coincidence."

"Right. Hear anything last night? Anything going on in your home before or after? Anything happening in the area?"

"We were and still are rather preoccupied with Mother passing away," she said, thinking that would set him straight and end his interrogation of her and the rest of her family.

"Right. I want to talk about your mother's death—"

Which instantly shot her back to her previous state. "What?" she demanded before he could even finish his sentence.

"Two deaths at the same address in less than a week."

"You've got to be kidding! You think they're *related*?" She rose from her chair. "Mom didn't want anyone to know she had cancer. But I ended up telling my family—afterwards." She took a big gulp of air and continued, "That woman out there have cancer? 'Cause that's not what I understood to be her cause of death!" She whirled and stalked out.

Becki fully understood the importance of the first forty-eight hours, however unpleasant it was to report to Detective Dumont, whose sole intent was to dig up dirt in a case that couldn't be anything other than murder.

"So, you arrive here in Langdon Hills and people drop like flies," he said.

"I beg your pardon!"

How could he know people dropped dead around her in Black Currant Bay too? The main difference between here and there being that, in Black Currant Bay, she was the one asking questions. Mind you, never in any official capacity.

"Tell me everything you can about what you've seen and heard since you've been here," he said.

"To tell the truth, something bothered me right off the bat—that Godmom was found with a pillow over her head."

"Ms. Green, in my experience dead bodies are found in the oddest positions, sometimes crowned with the strangest belongings."

"And in Godmom's case, you don't consider it an indication of foul play?"

"Who's interviewing who here?"

"Sorry."

"To answer your question, no. That's not how I read the scene at the time."

She noted his use of the phrase *'at the time.'*

"What have you observed since then?" he asked.

"The controversy of Godmom's will. No doubt you've taken a look at it. She left the bulk of her larger-than-expected estate to her grandkids and skipped a generation. Her eldest, Jerry, was visibly upset. Next day, he and his wife had a meeting with the lawyer. But most surprising, Detective, is that Tony is adopted or something. No one knew about it beforehand. Not even Tony. Weird, don't you think?"

"Not weird, but interesting." He tapped his hand steadily on the desk. Tap. Tap. Tap. "Anyway, here are my last few questions. For now. Did you recognize the victim when you saw her, and can you think of any connection she might have with this neighbourhood or with the Ferrero family?"

"Heavens, no!"

After the interview, she felt shaky. Must be from skipping breakfast. Because the session with Detective Dumont went as well as could be expected. To all appearances, he was a professional.

Cute too.

"Mom! Please."

She wobbled in the direction of the kitchen.

And French.

"God." She groaned. Or was that her stomach?

Don't tell me you didn't notice. I know you have this thing for accents.

"Detective Dumont doesn't have an accent, Mom."

But he's French. Dumont.

"Fifty years old, remember? Old enough to be his mom. Oh, hi, Gina!"

Chapter 13

Linda leaned back in the chair and crossed her slim legs. "Got a light?"

Rob shook his head. Now here was a very attractive woman. Mutton dressed as lamb, his mother would say, but attractive all the same. Not that she didn't work at it.

Linda sighed and reached for her purse. She pulled out a lighter and snapped it open. "That's the trouble with everyone these days. Nobody smokes."

"Mrs. Ferrero, I'd like to ask you a few questions."

"Call me Linda."

"Okay, Linda. You are staying at the house?"

"Yes," she said, blowing out smoke. "It's ghastly, but why pay for a hotel room?"

"Where were you last night, say, from ten o'clock on?"

"I was doing a facial from ten until about ten-thirty, then got dressed for bed. I didn't leave the bedroom until nine the next morning, if that's what you're getting at."

"Was your husband with you the whole time?"

"I don't know when he came in. But he slept in the bed beside me and was gone before I got up. He's an early riser. I'm not." She gave him a haughty smile.

Rob sighed. He saw all types, working for the force, and pampered women were not his favourite. At least she wasn't a cougar.

"Had you ever seen the victim before?"

Linda dragged on the cigarette. "I haven't seen her ever."

"I'm sorry—here's a photo."

Linda took it and squinted. "Not anyone I know." She handed it back.

"I guess that's all for now."

"You know where to find me." She gave the briefest smile of dismissal and then swept out.

Linda took the last of her cigarette out to the front porch. She was bothered.

That photo. She had spoken the truth to that handsome policeman. She had never seen the victim in that photo before. The woman didn't look like a secretary, but who could tell?

Who was the bitch? Did Jerry have anything to do with this? Was he up to his old tricks?

She sucked hard on the butt, then threw it on the stone sidewalk. She hadn't sensed any new woman and she was getting pretty good at telling the signs. Late nights at work…last minute business trips. This was something she would have to look into further. Sort through the Visa slips at home.

The cigarette butt gave one last smoulder and then petered out.

"Are you ready for me?"

Rob looked up and smiled at Gina. She stood at the door of the room, looking tentative and lovely.

"Come in. Sit down," he said.

"How are you, Rob?" Gina walked over to the guest chair and gracefully sat. Everything about Gina was graceful, just as he remembered. And he remembered a lot.

"I'm well," he said. "And you?"

She looked uncomfortable. *What a stupid thing to say,* he told himself. This was a murder investigation and she had seen the body.

He cleared his throat. "Tell me what you know about this."

"It isn't much," she said. "I went for a morning run and came back to find…well, you know. Tony and Aunt Mandy were already there. I don't ever remember seeing the woman before. And I didn't encounter anyone on my run."

"And last night?"

"I went to my room at nine and read for a while. Went to bed. Got up about six to run. I'm used to getting up early for the studio."

"There's nothing you can think of?"

She frowned and shook her head. "Nothing you wouldn't already have heard. You know about Grandmother. I'm sure Tony told you about being suspicious about her death. There was a lot of money at stake."

Rob nodded. "Yes, he said that."

"I just can't imagine who that woman was and why she was here. Nobody seems to have seen her before and this isn't exactly a town that attracts a lot of exotic strangers. It's mystifying."

"You think she's exotic?"

Gina looked up with a jerk. "Of course. That was an Armani she was wearing. And the bag was genuine Gucci. It must have cost three thousand dollars."

Three thousand dollars for a handbag? No ID inside? Rob couldn't believe it.

"So she certainly wasn't local," Gina was saying.

Rob looked across at her. He wanted to keep her in the room just so he could continue looking at her, but there didn't seem to be anything else he could think to ask.

"It's good to see you again," Rob said. "You're still close to Tony, I see."

Gina blushed. It made her look fifteen again.

"I wish you and me were still close," he said. *Good God, did he say that out loud?*

Gina started. "I think you blew that chance several years ago."

Rob went red. "I looked for you every evening for a week. They had already taken you home."

Gina looked down. "Mom figured it out immediately. She had me packing the next day and sent me to cousins in Vancouver."

Rob thought miserably about that last time they were together. He had been crazy about her—insanely, recklessly crazy. It had been so special in the forest by the oak tree…Gina so breathtakingly beautiful and innocent that he pressed her into something that went way too far…

"You could have phoned," Gina said. "You could have written." She sounded as hurt as if it had been yesterday.

The air in the room was suddenly stifling.

"I was afraid of what Tony would do," he said finally. He had been afraid too. You didn't mess around with a friend's cousin and come out of it with no consequences. Not back in those days. Not if it were Tony.

Gina's look softened. "Yes, there is that," she admitted. "We were awfully young."

"I don't think it would be any different now," he said. "I mean about Tony."

Gina smiled. "You seem to know him pretty well."

Rob smiled back. He loved to look at her. Every night he tuned to the Weather Network just to watch her on the screen. She was even lovelier in person. What a fool he'd been back then.

"He was always a tough guy. And a dare-devil. You're okay with what he's doing now?" Rob wondered about that. Gina didn't seem like the sort of girl who would tolerate rough stuff in her life.

"What do you mean?" Her face was puzzled.

"His work," Rob said. "His other work. You know."

"I *don't* know. What are you talking about?" Gina's eyes were troubled.

Good God, Rob thought. *She doesn't know. What do I do now?*

"Ask him," Rob said finally.

Gina would definitely ask him, but there was something else she was determined to do first. She went to the porch, palmed her cellphone and speed-dialled Holts.

"Lola, it's Gina from the Weather Network…Fine, how about you…? Good. Look, you know that gold Gucci handbag with the gold buckle—yes, that's the one—is it still available? No? Do you happen to know who purchased it…?"

Chapter 14

"Anyone feel claustrophobic like me?" Becki asked at lunch. "Gotta get out of here this afternoon." Her sanity depended on it.

"Me too," Linda said. "Five days and the only other place I've been outside this house is the cemetery."

"With all the rain we've had," Jerry said, "the courses have been too wet to golf."

"I got out jogging this morning. But look what happened."

Ian chimed in, "I should never have come in the first place."

"You got what you came for," Reggie grumbled.

"Maybe, but if it wasn't for the stupid interview with the detective this afternoon, I'd be on my way back to Toronto in a flash."

"And a whiff of perfume."

"For God's sake, Reggie!" Mandy said.

"Anyway," said Becki, "I've got to get out of here. Even if it's only temporarily. And on my drive into Langdon Hills, I saw this nifty-looking antique store. Anybody want to check it out with me? We could have an ice cream after."

She looked around. Nellie, at least, seemed to have perked her ears.

"Can Nellie come, Carla?"

"I'm taking her back to school this afternoon. She's missed enough classes already, right kiddo?"

Nellie pushed her plate away and slumped dramatically over the table.

"I'll see if I can find some little thing to bring back for you, Nellie," Becki said by way of consolation.

Nellie was sitting in the car already. Up in their suite, Carla said goodbye to Reggie. Gave him a quick kiss on the lips. "Good luck this afternoon."

"Just need to get in there and get it done."

"Be careful," she said.

"What's there to be careful about?"

"It's a *murder* investigation, Reggie. Cops want to pin it on somebody. Don't make yourself into a suspect."

"As if!"

"Dammit, you don't look like the sweet and innocent type. Take me seriously for once."

"Baby, would you love me if I was the sweet, innocent type?"

"I'm just saying. And…"

"Spit it out."

"There's a chance you'll recognize the victim."

"What?"

"Nellie claimed she came to the house."

"Who? The woman that died?"

Did his face drain of all colour? Or was it her imagination?

"Apparently, she came when we were gone and Nellie didn't answer the door."

"Well, if she didn't answer the goddamn door, how does she know who was there?"

"Shhh! No need to have a conniption. She peeked out the window."

"Who'd she see?"

"The woman in the picture Dumont showed us."

"And who was that?"

"Nellie doesn't know. And since I've never seen her before, neither do I. But maybe you've met her. Maybe she's come here before. Some saleswoman or something."

He scrunched his face. "Hmm…doubt it."

"Just warning you. Be on your toes. And on your best behaviour too. Don't want Dumont taking a dislike to you."

"Why the hell not?"

"Don't tell me you're that dense, Reggie."

He jutted his chin forward, splayed his large hands in the air. "What's not to like?"

Becki parked her car across the street from the antique store on the two-lane highway out of town. She climbed out. The sunshine on her skin felt glorious. Gina popped out of the passenger seat. Mandy and Linda climbed out the back.

In all likelihood, the building they were about to enter had once been a general store. It was painted red and white. It boasted a bay window and double glass doors with transoms above—all detailed with gingerbreading. On the wide, covered porch, Becki noted a Coca Cola cooler, a foot-pedalled sewing machine and a mannequin in vintage clothing. Out front sat a sandwich board that read: *Welcome to Gemma's Antiques & Old-fashioned Ice-cream Shop—Shakes, Sundaes, Cones.*

"Looking for anything in particular?" Gina asked. "Anything for Beautiful Things?"

"What could she possibly find here?" Linda peered through her sunglasses. "This place looks like a thrift shop, not a fine antiques establishment."

"Well, there's this trend to simplify," Becki said. "A return to basics. I bet I could pick up a gilt mirror or a wrought-iron bed. That kind of primitive element appeals to my clients in Black Currant Bay. The cottagers, at least."

"Shabby chic," said Mandy, nodding in agreement.

Linda nearly spit up. "Never put *shabby* and *chic* in the same sentence."

They crossed the road and entered the shop. Once inside, they all flipped their sunglasses to the tops of their heads. And in her characteristically disdainful way, Linda remarked the store's interior smelled dank. Her language was colourful. Becki hoped the proprietor was out of earshot. Thing was, Linda was right, except when passing by west-facing windows, where they caught streams of fresh air and shafts of light that set silver teapots, fancy stemware and lamps hung with crystal pendants gleaming.

They separated paths through the sprawl, sometimes browsing alone, sometimes together. Their groupings changed from time to time. But no matter how much time they spent looking, only the one person who poked in, around and behind everything, came out of the store with something besides an ice-cream cone.

"Don't you love it?" Becki enthused. She turned a bone china teacup painted with pink roses in the sunlight.

"A steal for eight dollars," she said. "You'd pay forty-five to fifty in Toronto. Amazing what you can find when you dig."

A faint sound of crickets chirped.

Gina reached into her purse. "Hello?" She turned away from the group and walked a few paces. "Yes...yes...that's great. Oh, thank you.

No, but I'll be in next week to look for evening wear, so put something by for me. The opera gala, so maybe something retro, over-the-top. Thanks a mil, Leslie. Bye."

She reached into her purse for a pen and small pad, then quickly wrote two words.

"Something important?" Linda asked.

"Actually, yes. I've got to get back to the house. You girls stay here. I'll catch a cab."

"What's up? Can you talk about it?" Becki was curious. Was this about Tony, or about the murder?

"Tell you all at dinner." Her hand flew up to catch the attention of the black and yellow cab across the street. It made a U-turn and stopped. She entered the back seat gracefully.

"What was that all about?" Linda stared after her.

"God knows." Carla shook her head. "Television people are all nuts."

"At least they have killer shoes," Linda said with approval.

When Gina arrived back at the house, Tony was pacing the front porch.

"Where did you go?" He seemed upset.

"Shopping with the girls. Is Rob about?"

"In the study. Look, you shouldn't go off like that without letting me know." He followed her into the house.

She stopped and turned. "Why ever not?"

Their eyes met and Gina reddened.

Tony looked uncomfortable. He glanced away. "It's not safe. There's a murderer about. And who knows what his motive is. At least let me know where you are."

So you can climb on your big white horse and rescue me, she thought to herself. In spite of everything, she smiled.

"I need to see Rob. Come with me—I have some news."

They found Dumont doing paperwork at the desk in the study. He was scowling. Obviously paperwork wasn't a huge favourite on his work hit parade.

"Can we come in?" Gina asked from the door.

"Sure." He brightened at the interruption. "Have a seat."

She sat down and leaned forward. Tony stood behind her.

"Hilary Best," she said with triumph.

"Who?"

"That's your mystery woman. Hilary Best."

Rob's mouth flew open. "How do you know?"

Gina leaned back in her chair and smiled. "The Gucci purse. Only two places in Toronto carry them and they only get one-of-a-kind each. I phoned Holt Renfrew first, but that one was purchased by Lainy Andrews. I know her. It couldn't be her. So I phoned the Gucci store next. They checked their records and just got back to me. Hilary Best bought it two weeks ago."

Rob muttered a curse. "Did she, now? You know her?"

"I know of her. Never been introduced to her, but she was pointed out to me from a distance. One of two socialite sisters. Canada's version of Nicky and Paris Hilton, but Hilary and Andrea spat like cat and dog. She's also the ex of that guy who made all the money in diamonds up north. She's got this reputation for being somewhat of a..." Gina wondered if she could say the word out loud. "...cougar."

Tony snorted behind her.

Rob's mouth flew open. Then it shut. He flushed. "Didn't look old enough for that."

Well, well. Rob was familiar with the club scene lingo. After all, he was single. Still, it made her wonder about the women he dated.

Gina looked at him directly and tried hard to keep her mind on topic. "She'd had a recent facelift. Couldn't you tell?"

Rob shook his head. "You found this out because of a handbag?"

"And I confirmed her description. It's her. I'd bet my last cannoli."

"Why did they even give you this information? Isn't that breaking privacy rules or something?"

Gina smiled. "They break the rules, as you put it, all the time. See, if I'm going to a gala or media night, I need to know what I'm wearing is exclusive, so I don't run into anyone else with the same thing on. We get to know the sales clerks pretty well. They'll tell us who buys what so we don't get embarrassed in public."

She could hear Tony chuckling quietly behind her. "It's important." Gina turned and scowled at him.

"For someone only half Italian, you sure got all the fashion genes." Tony shook his head. "You women are kooky. Catch some guy caring whether another dude is wearing the same shit."

Rob laughed. "Catch some guy even noticing."

"Stop being nasty." Gina wouldn't look at them now. Of all the stupid male egos. She had solved the puzzle. They were miffed at that, for sure.

Rob reached for the phone. "I'll check it out just the same. Any idea where she lives?"

"Toronto," Gina said. "Probably a condo in Yorkville or Harbourfront. Most of the ex-wives live there."

Again, Rob shook his head. "Thanks, Gina. This should speed things up."

They turned to leave. Rob started punching numbers into his phone.

Out in the hall, Tony said, "Let's go for a walk. I need to get out of here."

"When I feel that way, I go shopping. Just like today." She smiled sweetly. God, she could be a bitch at times. Tony didn't seem to notice. He appeared deep in thought. They walked off the property and along the tree-lined sidewalk.

"Rob interviewed Mom this morning. She couldn't help him much, of course."

"Was she okay about it?"

Tony laughed. "Oh yeah. She loves all this attention. At one point, she told Rob how he should try Internet dating sites to find someone special. But he really needed to buy new clothes first."

Gina whooped. "I'll bet he loved that. The big detective lectured on his love life by a suspect."

"It's pretty hard to keep Mom on topic," Tony said.

They walked in silence for several minutes. The neighbourhood had the shabby look of old gentility. Bushes were overgrown and the sidewalk was cracked and shifting. Gina had to watch her heels, even though these Ferragamo's were pretty flat for her.

"Look, I need to talk to you about this cousin thing," Tony said out of the blue.

Gina nearly tripped. Tony caught her arm just in time.

"I know this isn't the best time, with this investigation going on and all, but I need to let you know how I feel about it all."

Her heart skipped. "You mean about being adopted?"

He nodded. "That and other things. I thought about it, and I don't really mind about being adopted. Mom and Dad raised me well, and I never felt unloved or anything. No, I'm actually happy about it, which is perhaps unusual." He paused.

Unusual perhaps, but not unexpected, given the circumstances, Gina thought. *He's going to bring it out in the open now. What am I going to do? What am I going to say?*

What he said next was unexpected. "We're not ortho-cousins. Did you ever take anthropology at university?"

Gina shook her head.

"Ortho-cousins are cousins whose mothers were sisters, or whose fathers were brothers. In other words, their related parents share the same gender. Cross-cousins are cousins where the related parents are brother and sister." Tony paused to let that sink in. "I've been doing some research lately. In many cultures cross-cousins are allowed to marry but ortho-cousins aren't."

"That's crazy," Gina said. "Surely there's no genetic difference."

"True, but they didn't know that back when they made the rules. Genetics wasn't a science then."

Tony stopped to pick a dandelion from between the sidewalk crack.

"Look, Gina, I'm crazy about you. I always have been. I couldn't ever dare tell you because it wasn't right. My God, it even seemed like incest. Can you imagine how I felt about that? Me, your older cousin who was supposed to protect you from all the other guys? And all this time I...well, I was just as bad in what I was thinking and feeling. Hiding it from you. Hiding it from everyone like I was some kind of monster."

Gina stopped walking, her heart in her throat.

"But I'm not your cousin now," he said. "At least, we're not related by blood. And I need to know..."

He looked at her intently and in such a way that was both hard and soft at the same time and she thought her heart would stop.

"Gina, I need to know if you might possibly be able to see me in the same way. Not as a cousin, but as something more."

She didn't know what to say.

He placed his hands on her shoulders. "Gina?"

She was in his arms the next second. After that, there didn't seem a reason to say a word.

When Jerry passed them in the car, he nearly drove off the road.

Chapter 15

"You're my last interview here, Reggie," Rob said, shaking Reggie's hand. It had been a long day. "And first off, I want to thank you for allowing me to interview your family and houseguests so comfortably at the scene like this."

"It's fine."

"I'll be popping in to see your neighbours on either side, then handling the rest of the investigation from the station."

The two men walked together from the doorway to the desk and took seats on either side.

"You heading up the investigation?" Reggie asked.

"Only major crimes detective in Langford Hills."

Reggie then asked if he was calling in the Ontario Provincial Police or the Royal Canadian Mounted Police.

"So far, it's not a joint operation," Rob replied, trying hard not to let it show how much Reggie's question pissed him off.

"I get it. None of my business."

"Let's get to it. And then I'll be out of your hair. Recognize the victim?"

Rob handed over the photo. He watched Reggie's face. Even when a person forces himself to remain blank, some expression is unavoidable. Unless he's a master spy or something. There was a perceptible widening of Reggie's eyes.

"Nah."

"Funny, I have a lead on who this is, and you were seen outside," he looked down at the desk at the notes spread out in front of him, "the Green Hills Motor Court with a woman who looked just like her."

Reggie remained silent.

"Rethinking your answer?"

"All the damn thinking in the world won't change my answer, bud." Reggie's tone was abrasive.

Early days. Could be Ian was lying about seeing Reggie with the victim. Or maybe Ian thought it was the victim, but it was really some other woman. Or some other man. First conflicting witness testimony in the case. Means I'm getting somewhere.

"So, Reggie, where were you between the hours of 10:00 last night and 7:00 this morning?"

"Had a nightcap right here in this room, actually, then went upstairs to bed. That's it, that's all." Reggie placed both hands on his hips, thus increasing the span of his body. "Exactly like my wife told you this morning."

"Only thing I asked Carla this morning was if she noticed anything unusual."

When Nellie squeezed through the back door into the kitchen, Aunt Becki asked, "How was school?"

"Okay, I guess."

"No problem on the way home?" Mom asked.

"Nope."

A few times during her walks home, Andy, a stupid bully in her class, had ripped up her artwork or whistled in her ear or flipped her skirt. But not today.

"Chocolate chip cookies and a glass of milk for a snack?" Mom asked.

"Yes, please."

"And, sweetie, Aunt Becki has something for you." Mom's face was shiny.

It made Nellie feel good seeing Mom like that. "What?"

In answer, Aunt Becki plunked a square package in front of her spot at the table.

"Brown paper packages tied up with string," Mom sang. "You can open it, hon."

So Nellie tugged both ends until the bow loosened and the cord slipped off. Turned the package over and separated the paper where it was Scotch-taped together. "A book."

"Can you read any of the words in the title?" Aunt Becki asked.

"The...the..." She used her finger to help guide her through the letters, but the next word was way too hard.

"The Island of Adventure," Mom said, looking delighted, even though Nellie hadn't managed to read it. "By Enid Blyton."

"It may be a bit old for you, but I'll read you some while I'm here and I'm sure your Mom will want to read it with you too."

"Aunt Becki and I both read the whole series when we were—"

Aunt Becki jumped in. "It's a collectible now."

"Good?" Nellie asked.

"Absolutely," Mom and Aunt Becki said together.

Becki's stomach growled. She went outside for some fresh air and quiet before supper.

Jerry was making the evening meal tonight. He kept yelling at Ian, "How do you...? What goes in the...?"

The sky was coral pink as she wandered down the lawn and stood under the old maple. Rather than look out toward the police tape, the alley, the forest and the setting sun beyond, she faced the house and marvelled at the rapid changes in the light and how it affected the tint of the brick and reflections in the windows.

"Raindrops on roses and whiskers on kittens..."

Ah, Carla was out, enjoying the remnants of the day. Becki looked around. The yard was empty. *Where is she exactly?*

"...a few of my favourite things."

Her voice carried beautifully in the stillness of dusk. Becki turned and walked to the alley. She looked south, but there was no one along its gloomy length. She twisted and looked in the other direction, past the taped off section, and there she saw Carla.

Carla was zigzagging along the gravel dragging one foot.

"What's wrong?" Becki cried.

"When the dog bites..."

Her heart began to pound. She was at Carla's side in seconds. Blood, still dripping from Carla's nose, had stiffened the material of the front of her blouse, which was ripped open at the neck; one of her eyes was swollen shut, and the skin around the other was mottled brown and purple; her hair was matted with what Becki also feared was blood.

"When I'm feeling sad..."

Becki put her arm around her, but Carla kept trudging forward. To stop her, Becki had to step right into her path, look directly into her eyes and whisper, "Carla, we're going to the hospital, okay?"

Rather than wait at the Langford Hills Hospital—which resembled a small clinic in her mind—while the doctor examined Carla, and before calling anyone at the house, Becki headed to the police station two doors down. By now it was dark. She wasn't sure Detective Dumont would be there after his long day at the house, but there would be someone on duty.

She pulled open a heavy glass door, climbed a few stairs, opened another door, crossed a linoleum floor, and waited for service at what looked like a Sears Catalogue counter, except the female clerk who eventually came to see what Becki wanted wore a uniform. And a gun.

"Help you?"

"Detective Dumont in?" Becki asked.

"Ask what this is about?"

"A case...A case he's on."

"Which one?"

"Murder on Hawthorne."

"I'll get him."

The policewoman lumbered into the back and disappeared down a hallway. Becki was pleased Dumont was still there. While she waited, she tried not to look like a maniac for the sake of the young boy seated on a bench to one side. Finally, she saw Rob Dumont appear at the back of the room. He walked toward the dividing counter.

"Ms. Green. What's up?"

"Another attack."

"When?"

"Just found Carla Williamson in back of the house. Nellie's mom. Brought her next door to the hospital. She's beaten bad."

"She say anything?"

"Who did it, you mean?"

Dumont nodded.

"No. When the nurses asked her, she just kept repeating, 'In the face.' But she's hit everywhere. She's limping—"

Swinging open the gate in the counter, he said, "Let's go."

Chapter 16

Carla was a mess. That much Rob could see. It hurt him just looking at her. The nurse had given her a load of painkillers and she wasn't very sentient.

"Carla, who did this to you?"

"Didn't see."

The nurse was hovering. She looked formidable. "Inspector, I insist. We need to prep her."

"You didn't see your attacker?" It didn't make sense. She was hit in the face, among other places. She must have seen someone.

The nurse pushed him out of the examining room. He'd have to get a uniform to come guard her. He left to use his cellphone outside.

When he returned, Becki was sitting in a chair by the wall, drinking out of a paper cup. Her eyes were anxious. "Did she say anything?"

Rob sat down next to her. "She says she didn't see him."

"But that doesn't make sense," Becki said.

"I know. She has to be protecting someone. Don't know if it's just her attacker or the killer too."

Becki gasped. "You don't think they're the same person?"

Linda and Jerry came rushing down the hall.

Linda was out of breath. She looked like she was ready to host an evening cocktail party in that get-up. *Mutton dressed as lamb,* Rob thought again.

"I've ordered roses," Linda said with satisfaction. "Pink ones. They didn't have yellow."

Rob looked at her as if she'd spoken in Swahili. What the hell had roses to do with anything?

"Ian's parking the car. How is she?" Jerry asked.

"Pretty beat up," Becki said. "But they think she'll be all right, as long as there's no internal damage. She's going for X-rays or MRIs—whatever they do now."

"That bastard Reggie." Linda almost spit the words.

"You think Reggie did this?"

"Of course, he did. He's the wife-beater type. Good-looking, thinks a lot of himself and a total failure at everything he tries. So he takes it out on someone weaker. Believe me, I know the type."

Everyone looked at Jerry.

"No, no! I don't mean like Jerry. Don't be ridiculous. I just know. From before...in my childhood."

Everyone stared at her. She shifted nervously from foot to high-heeled foot. "What are you looking at?"

"Do you know this for sure or are you just surmising? Has Carla said anything to you?"

Linda shook her head.

"Has she said anything to anyone else?"

Both Becki and Jerry shook their heads.

"Do we know this has happened before? Have any of you seen any signs of bruising on Carla that might be indicative?"

Linda and Jerry shook their heads this time. Becki did not, Rob noted. He looked right at her and crossed his arms.

"I'm not sure," Becki said carefully. "There are times I've thought it odd—the things she'd wear. Turtlenecks when it was too hot and long sleeves. She didn't wear her favourite dinner dress once when she had the chance and I couldn't figure out why. The excuse she made was nonsense. And once I saw these marks on her upper arms that looked like thumbprints. She said she'd hit the wall funny, but you don't get marks on both sides by doing that."

"Just like I said." Linda was triumphant.

Rob sat, thinking. It looked like a simple case of wife-beating...what a terrible way to put it. Simple made it sound ordinary or banal, when, as a man, he thought this was one of the most despicable things another man could do. *What a terrible world we live in,* Rob thought bitterly.

"Reggie is a bastard. I bet he killed the other woman too. Probably having an affair with her, the son-of-a-bitch." Linda was on a soapbox.

"He was having an affair with someone. I don't know if it was her,"

Jerry said. "Ian saw him at the motel with a woman."

There was a sharp intake of breath from Linda. "What hotel?"

"The one on the edge of town, the Green Hills something."

"Why didn't you tell me? Why didn't Ian?"

Jerry just shrugged.

"Did you know about this?" Linda turned to Rob. She sounded personally outraged.

Rob nodded. "Ian told me. We're checking it out."

All this time, Becki had been quiet. She spoke up now. "You can't be sure Reggie killed that other woman."

"What do you mean?" Rob asked

"I know what you mean," Jerry said. "If he was the killer, he wouldn't have used a bat. Reggie would have used his bare hands."

Ian had not told the police everything. Yes, he had confessed to Dumont about seeing a woman with Reggie, but he neglected mentioning the woman was familiar. That would have been the right thing to do, of course, but Ian had plans of his own. Besides, he liked to plant a few wild seeds and watch them grow. Let the police find out who the mystery dame was—that was their job. Ian would guard his own thoughts, which were both puzzling and disturbing. For Ian had seen someone who shouldn't be there. Rather, someone who surprised him; a person who had no reason to be in town at this time. He frowned, wondering what to do about it. At last, he pulled the cellphone from his pocket. The number was there in his speed dial. He stared at it, and then called.

Gina looked up from her cellphone. She felt like she'd been hit by a truck.

"What is it?" Tony asked. They were drinking takeout coffees, walking home.

"That was Becki. Carla is in hospital. She's been beaten badly."

Tony cursed. "Let's go," he said. He looked on high alert.

"I can't. I have to get home for Nellie. Becki asked me to just now. Nellie is at a friend's. Someone has to stay until she gets home." Gina's voice was breaking. "You go."

He shook his head. "I'm not leaving you and Nellie. Not now."

They walked quicker. "The killer is close, isn't he?" She shivered.

Tony's look was dark. "Yes, but I don't know if the killer did this to Carla."

"You think it's two separate people?" That was too horrible. Gina could hardly bear the thought—two dangerous people running lose.

"I just said I don't know. But the killer is close, so I'm not taking any chances."

Gina wondered what he meant by not taking any chances. He looked deep in thought, a million miles away. What was he planning to do?

She decided to take the plunge. "Tony, do you have a gun with you?"

He looked up, startled. "Why on earth would you ask that?"

Evasion. That was no answer. He did have a gun, then. She forced herself to tread deeper into the water.

"It was something Rob said by mistake. A little slip...something he thought I would already know. He looked red and back-peddled immediately." Gina watched Tony closely. His face had completely shut down. "Look, I don't know what you're doing or what you're into, but if it has something to do with this murder, you've got to tell me."

Tony snapped back to the present. "It has nothing to do with this murder."

"You're sure?" She didn't know whether to believe him.

"Positive."

"Does Rob know this?"

"Yes. He asked the same thing."

Gina felt herself exhale. "So are you going to tell me what the gun is all about?"

A pause. They were nearly at the house.

"No." His voice was low.

Gina's feet wouldn't move. She couldn't feel the ground. She felt as if the world had suddenly lost all gravity and her body was up there floating, spinning around in space.

This is what betrayal is like. This is what it feels like to have the one man you trust turn into a stranger.

It took her a full minute to talk.

"Well, I guess that's it then," she said. She ran up the steps to the house and didn't look back.

Tony stood on the sidewalk looking after her. Damn Dumont. Damn him to hell. He knew the score. He knew the deal on secrecy. Why the hell would he think Gina could know?

Unless Rob did it on purpose. Unless the son-of-a-bitch wanted Gina himself and knew that this was a way to split them up before they even got started. Tony felt anger twist in him. Giving away cover was a serious offence. He could have Rob's badge for this. Tony vaulted up the steps to the house and flung open the door, slamming it against the porch wall.

Chapter 17

Nellie knew right after Mr. Spenser pulled up to the curb in front of her house that something was wrong because normally she let herself in and Mom would be waiting in the living room or the kitchen. But tonight, before she finished thanking Mr. Spenser, Cousin Gina stepped out onto the porch. And even though Gina waved, she looked worried.

Gina came to her and hugged her tightly. "Let's go in." To Abigail's dad, she said, "Bye. Thank you."

"What's going on?" Nellie asked.

After closing the door behind them, Gina said, "Let's sit in the living room before you go up to bed."

"Where's Mom?"

They walked into the room. Aunt Mandy and Cousin Tony were there.

"Why don't you sit down," Aunt Mandy said.

Even if it started with the word *why*, it wasn't a question. So Nellie sat in her favourite chair, the one that was good for reading. "Where's Mom?"

"That's what we want to talk to you about," Gina said. She looked at Tony and he looked back at her.

Nellie knew it was going to be worse than when Father found out she spilled orange juice in his truck. He'd wanted to get out his belt and punish her, but Mom said it was just an accident and partly her fault for letting her have a juice box while they were out running errands. And not to take it out on their daughter.

"Your Mom's in the hospital," Tony explained.

"The doctors there are looking after her," Gina said.

"She'll be fine," Aunt Mandy said.

Nellie rubbed her hands on the sides of her jeans. "Can I go to the hospital and see her?"

"Maybe in the morning."

"Probably."

"Everything's going to be all right, dear."

"Father?"

They all looked surprised.

"We don't know, dear."

Sometimes he was gone all night. Not as scary as Mom being in the hospital. "Do I still go to school tomorrow?"

"Not if you don't want to," Gina said.

Nellie's lip quivered.

"Do you think you can start getting ready for bed now, hon?" asked Gina. "If I help?"

"What about Mom's goodnight kiss?" Nellie tried to get off the chair like she knew she was supposed to, but her legs got tangled up and she tripped. All three grown-ups reached out to catch her, but she didn't fall. Or cry. She thought she might make it all the way up the stairs without any tears because she almost never cried in front of people. Except it felt like an entire ocean was pushing against her eyeballs from inside. She let out a howl. "I want Mom!"

Her aunt and two cousins rushed toward her. Nellie knew they'd all put their arms around her and try to comfort her. But she turned to Gina and buried her face in her cousin's stomach.

Becki called the house to see how Nellie was doing and also to pass along the last thing Detective Dumont had said before leaving the hospital. *One thing for sure, tell everyone in the Ferrero family that no one, including Ferrero houseguests, leaves until this case is sorted out.*

While on the phone, after assuring Becki she'd managed to settle Nellie, Gina had passed along her own piece of startling news. Her mother and father had cut short their vacation, flown all day and were now heading to Langdon Hills in an airport limo.

In the meantime, Becki was trying to find a comfortable position in one of the plastic chairs in Carla's hospital room. Jerry, Linda and Ian were still around somewhere. Maybe getting chocolate glazed donuts from a Tim Hortons, if there was one in Langdon Hills. But Becki wanted to make sure Carla didn't wake up to an empty room. She was pretty sure the guard outside the door wouldn't be a reassuring presence.

Becki knew she couldn't sleep even if she did find a position she could hold longer than five minutes. Some people could sleep sitting up, some couldn't. When she worked in Toronto, there was this annoying co-worker who bragged that after she closed up whenever she worked late, she got on the subway at Eglinton and slept until the train stopped at her station—North York Centre—and she never, ever missed her stop.

"Ahhh!" Carla's body jerked under the thin blanket covering her. Her better eye opened.

"It's all right, Carla," Becki soothed. "Sleep if you want. Everything's fine. Sleep."

But Carla turned her head left, then right, and pushed herself up against the headboard. She was bandaged and her leg was in a cast, but she wasn't attached to any tubes or lines, so Becki adjusted the pillow behind her back. "How're you feeling?" she asked.

Carla looked at her and asked her own question. "Nellie?"

"At home. Gina tucked her into bed. With Macho."

Carla nodded.

"You checked out okay, Carla. No life-threatening injuries. Thank God. Dr. Henry will let you go home tomorrow. But he wants you to sleep it off tonight, okay?"

Carla mumbled past her cracked lip. "Okay."

"Detective Dumont was here."

That made Carla tense.

"Wanted to know who did it."

"You tell him?" Carla asked, chewing her bottom lip.

"No, you're the only one who can. We don't know who attacked you. I found you in the alley not far from where that woman was murdered, so we're all scared you may have run into the killer. And maybe you would recognize him if you saw him again. Got a guard outside your door and everything."

Carla glanced toward the hall.

Becki knew what she wanted to ask next was a touchy subject. "Unfortunately, we're also wondering if maybe Reggie did it." She paused for a moment. "He's nowhere to be found. You'd think he'd be here, with his wife in the hospital. I mean…if he knew."

"He knows, all right," Carla said, her single eye blazing. "Bastard!"

Becki hesitated because she wasn't exactly Dr. Phil. "Wanna talk?"

"I told him if he ever hit me again, we were done. *Over.*" Her one eye rounded in terror.

"Nellie will be fine," Becki said, acknowledging what Carla needed to hear. "Mandy's there. Gina. Tony. They've been warned it might have been Reggie who beat you. There's no way he'll get near her tonight. He'd have to get through Tony first."

Carla sighed. "I tell myself he's just taking out his frustrations. Not thinking. He can be so sweet the next day, you know."

"Suppose," Becki mumbled. *Not the time for a lecture on the cycle of abuse.*

"But now? I'm sure he hates me." Carla began to sob. "I tell him I'll leave if he keeps on hitting me. And what does he do? Beats me to a bloody pulp. And he never hit me in the face before. I pleaded for him to stop."

Jerry took a turn sitting with his baby sister, but couldn't be long because Linda was waiting in the car. Meanwhile, Becki walked the silent hall, feeling badly for Carla and for all the poor souls who were patients in the darkened rooms of Langdon Hills Hospital.

She was pretty tired herself and wasn't paying attention. Just walking. Ended up outside the tiny, glass-walled waiting room near the entrance and saw Ian pacing inside. He had his phone to his ear. *Aren't cellphones prohibited in hospitals?*

She'd made her calls to the house from the pay phone in the foyer.

She was about to go in and see if there was a halfway decent magazine to read in the pile on the coffee table when she stopped. *Is there a full moon out or something? Ian is shouting.*

"Andrew, listen to me! You're not doing this to me. You going to walk away from two million dollars?"

And while his face flushed redder and redder, Becki worried every single man in Langdon Hills was transforming into the darkest version of himself.

Chapter 18

Tony's cellphone vibrated. He reached for it and barked, "Hello! Yeah...yeah. Of course I'm not leaving."

He listened for a minute and then his temper got the better of him.

"Dumont, you son-of-a-bitch, what the hell did you tell Gina?"

A pause. "Sorry about that. I thought she knew."

"Like hell. You know the rules. You put me at risk."

"Sorry, man. I messed up."

Tony gritted his teeth. "You did this on purpose, didn't you? Trying to cut me out so you can run in? I know you've got a history with her." Tony was barely holding it in. Just because they'd been childhood friends didn't give Dumont any rights to her now.

"She told you about that? Shit, Tony, that was almost fifteen years ago and you know what she was like back then—a living angel. I couldn't help myself. It was just one time. Okay, maybe that makes it sound worse, but I feel like shit about it."

Tony could scarcely breathe. What the fuck was this about?

"You never told me," he said coldly.

"Of course I didn't tell you. You're her cousin. You would have killed me."

Tony's head was spinning. His brain started to calculate. *How old was she then? Fifteen? Bastard! The fucking bastard!*

He swung back his arm and pitched the cell as far as he could.

Gina came out of Nellie's room and down the stairs. She went to the kitchen and slid into a chair. "I finally got her settled," she said, pushing a stray lock of hair behind her ear. "Poor little thing." Mother in the hospital, father missing in action and probably a murderer. It was too much.

"I made some tea. Want a cup?" Mandy started to pour. She did it elegantly, without spilling a drop.

Gina had to smile. Whenever she poured tea, there was always a ring left on the table. Why couldn't the engineers who put a man on the moon invent a teapot that didn't leak?

"I've made up the blue room for your parents. They should be here soon."

Gina brightened. "Thanks, Aunt Mandy. That was thoughtful."

Mandy smiled. "Figured they'd need the bigger room to spread out. I'm sure they'll come laden with a whole bunch of presents like they always do."

They sat in companionable silence. Finally, some peace from all the turmoil. Gina let her mind go blank. It was such a relief.

"You'll be glad to see your mom," Mandy said.

Gina sighed. "I've missed her. But I'm glad she's been out of this. She can't be a suspect now."

"There is that," Mandy said quietly.

Gina looked over at her aunt and felt comfort. Hard to believe she and her son didn't share the same blood. They were so alike in temperament.

"Where's Tony?" It was the most natural thing in the world for her to ask, but Gina immediately regretted it. Why did she care so much? How could she trust a man who wouldn't tell her the truth about himself?

"Out back pacing the lawn. I think he's brooding. He was always like that as a little boy. Far too serious. Don't you remember? Or maybe not…you're younger." Mandy looked up from her tea. "You two have a fight?"

Gina pursed her lips.

"Aunt Mandy, what do you know about Tony's job?"

There was a pregnant pause. Mandy gazed right into her eyes and her look was candid. "Which one do you mean, dear?"

Several minutes later, Gina stepped off the back porch. The moonlight was bright and the stars twinkled. She walked about fifty paces toward the trees, then stopped. She steeled her resolve.

Tony was bent over at the waist about ten feet away. He hadn't turned at her approach, which was unusual.

"What are you doing?" she said.

Tony looked up from the ground, startled. His eyes narrowed and then he scowled. "Looking for my cell," he said. "I dropped it."

Gina raised an eyebrow. Funny place to be dropping a cellphone. She pulled her own out of her pocket. She tapped a few times. Within seconds a buzzing sound came from behind her left shoulder. She walked over and picked up the humming cellphone.

"Looks a bit cracked," she said. "You must have dropped it a fair distance." She handed it over to him.

"Son-of-a-bitch," he muttered, pocketing the thing. "This day just goes from bad to worse."

Gina watched his face and actually felt sorry for him. He looked lost.

"Aunt Mandy says you're brooding. How come?"

Tony fixed his eyes on her. He looked undecided and then finally it all burst out.

"Dumont told me a little tidbit about you two from way back when. I think you were maybe fifteen?"

Oh shit. She felt her face go white.

"Did you consent?"

"Of course not," she answered quickly, and then regretted it, hesitating over the next words. "Or at least—it happened so fast, and I didn't know what he was going to do exactly." *Probably it happened to a great many girls this way the first time.*

"The fucking bastard," Tony mumbled. One fist hit the palm of his other hand repeatedly. "I'll tear him apart."

Now Gina was worried. "Don't be ridiculous. It was a long time ago and he was gentle about it. I didn't suffer any permanent damage. Just let it go."

"You think I can let that go?" He looked dangerous now, like a stalking panther. "You think I can let him get away with this? The lying, sneaking bastard! All this time, pretending to be a friend of mine." Anger rocked him.

Gina's eyes went wide. "I get it now. Oh, I get it all right. You're mad it wasn't you the first time, back then. You were my cousin, Tony. And that makes it all kinds of creepy, doesn't it?"

Tony went rigid. She saw the horror cross his face and knew she'd hit the mark.

Tony ran a hand through his hair. "Bloody hell." He was returning to his old self quickly, the man she knew and loved. "Bloody hell, you're right. I am way out of line and I can't help myself. You've got to understand, though. You can't help what you feel. You can only try to hide it, control it, subdue the beast. I did that, as best I could."

Gina's heart caught in her throat. This was an amazing confession, way beyond his earlier one.

"I was young, and I went through hell wanting you in that way. Wondering what it would be like, night after night...hating myself." He stopped abruptly.

She thought she might faint. He stared at her expectantly. His eyes were dark pools.

"Say something. Crissake, Gina, say something or change the subject. Don't leave me hanging here."

Gina sucked in air. Now or never. "Okay, this is different. This is different and a half. Your mom told me to watch the movie *True Lies*. That's all she said. Thing is, I'd already seen it." She waited for his reaction.

His eyes moved away and then his face shut down. He folded his arms across his chest. She was reminded of that famous statue, Bernini's David—the fixed, determined set to the mouth, the rigid, contorted body.

She continued. "Last month when you went to Dubai. You weren't in Dubai, were you?"

He looked over, measuring. He made no move and said nothing.

"So you weren't. Don't worry. I won't make you answer." She stood in the dappled moonlight sorting out the words to say next. It was important they were the right words. Both their futures would depend upon it. She said them carefully.

"All these years your mom stood it. I guess I can try to do the same."

He moved like a wildcat, pulling her to him. His mouth covered hers and she was gone.

Chapter 19

It turned out to be one of those autumn mornings that had a slight mist to it, either because the air was cooler than the earth or vice versa. Thus, the reds and yellows of the trees, the blue of the sky and the paint colours on the trim and signs of Langdon Hills' stores were all muted. Now, as Becki avoided the dew on the grass on either edge of the sidewalk, she couldn't help thinking it must be tragic for Carla to be headed to the police station to officially press charges against her husband.

For the second time in as many days, Becki turned and walked up the path to the police station doors, this time in less of a panic, and this time accompanying Carla, who—if you were to go by the scowl on her face and the twitch of the fingers of her right hand—was feeling determination tinged with nerves.

Always searching for a way to lighten things up, Becki read out loud the lettering on the cop shop's exterior door. Generally a thorough reader of printed instructions, she'd missed the sign on her first visit due to anxiousness to get to Detective Dumont. "No Firearms," she read. "Please leave firearms and ammunition in your vehicle."

"No way. They've got to be kidding." Carla showed just a hint of a smile.

"Uh...married to a cop, so I can vouch for the fact they tend to have an odd sense of humour, but I don't think that sign's meant to be humorous."

"But it is," Carla insisted.

"Some dumb-ass criminals out there," Becki said, only to regret it so much she could kick herself.

Inside, Detective Dumont was expecting them. He talked to them together first, then with Carla alone. When it was over, Carla hobbled out of Detective Dumont's office, her walking cast an obvious handicap.

"You okay?" Becki asked.

"Rather not talk about it."

And so Becki drove her home in what she hoped was companionable silence.

Later, back in her guest bedroom at the house, Becki explained to Karl over the phone, "So you see, I'm pretty much stuck here."

"Looks like it."

"Miss you."

"Miss you too."

"How much?" she asked, needing reassurance.

"So much I gained five pounds."

"What? I'm away for a week and you *gain* weight. You're supposed to pine away."

"Miss your healthy vegetarian cooking."

"You're teasing me now."

"Serious. Can hardly remember the last time I had one of your chocolate protein shakes for breakfast."

"Oh?"

"Thank the Lord."

"Smarten up, Karl!"

He laughed.

"I've got real trouble here."

"Sorry. How's Carla?"

"Recovering."

"That's good."

"Nellie's glad to have her home, even if their reunion seemed awkward at first."

"Awkward?"

"Took a while for Nellie to get used to the new Carla. I guess she looked pretty scary, what with the leg cast, the bandages and two black eyes."

"Goddamn Reggie! And we don't know the half of what he put her through. On average, a domestic victim experiences thirty-five assaults before ever calling the police."

"That's gross, Karl."

"As you know, sometimes we're not called soon enough. Or, hate to say it, we're not effective in protecting the victim. In Ontario alone, between 2002 and 2007, one-hundred forty-two women were *murdered* by their partner."

"That makes twenty-three women a year, Karl."

"Crazy, huh?"

"You sure you got your figures straight?"

"Unfortunately."

"This morning I was remembering *our* wedding." She smiled. "Love you, Karl."

"Love you back..." Just before hanging up, she thought she heard him add, "...sweetheart."

After calling her half-sister, Anne, to see if their store, Beautiful Things, was still standing, then her friends, Kathleen and France, Becki brought all her dirty clothes down to the basement and threw them in the washing machine in one load. No separating the darks from the colours from the whites. No waiting for a full load in order be kind to the environment. Dire circumstances. But she did choose the cold water wash option.

Then she joined Gina's just-arrived mom in Godmom's bedroom, of all places. Anna had announced earlier the least she could do for everyone while she was here was sort through her mother's closet and box up the clothes to give to Goodwill.

"Hey, Anna," Becki said.

"Hello again, dear."

The song "My Favorite Things" tinkled in the air around them.

"So can I help you now?" Becki asked.

"No. Thank you. I've managed to shoo you and everyone else away so far. Haven't been here to support you all up 'til now. Let me do this."

Although her tone was firm, Becki noticed Anna's hand holding the music box trembled. She sensed pending tears. Perhaps she'd best give the woman more time to grieve. "I'll go make you tea to sip while you work. The other day I bought Crème Brûlée Rooibos, and it's delicious."

"Sure, love."

Several minutes later, Becki returned with a tray. On it a teapot, two cups and saucers—one set was the one she bought at the antique store—a strainer, a little pitcher of milk and a plate with several of the chocolate chip cookies Carla baked yesterday. "I'll set it here for whenever you're ready," she said and found a spot on the nightstand.

"Does smell good," Anna said. "What kind of tea did you say it was? Herbal?"

"Yes. And it tastes like caramel." *Anna's skin looks caramel, which is what cruising does for your average Canadian. Long ago, her hair turned prematurely white. She'd probably look younger if she dyed it, but not as distinctive,* thought Becki.

"Pour me a little now, won't you? And you'll join me, of course."

"Notice the two cups?"

Once they were seated on the edge of the bed, Becki said, "I'm sorry about your mom. And Carla."

"Not to mention the poor woman Mandy found out back. A murder. God help us."

"One good thing—the police can't suspect you or Gord, or hold you here in the house against your will. You weren't even in town when it happened."

"I'm not sure that exonerates us. There's always murder by proxy."

Becki got up from her seat on the edge of the bed and paced the room, all the while nursing her teacup. When she put it down on the tray, she offered, "How about I gather up Godmom's meds and drop them off at the pharmacy or the hazardous goods depot or do whatever you're supposed to do with drugs?"

"That'd help," Anna admitted.

Becki grabbed a small box from the pile of cardboard containers, opened the tiny drawer in the nightstand and took inventory: a flashlight, a notepad, a pencil, a pen—no, two pencils and a pen—the August edition of *Chatelaine*, a soft-cover book of crosswords, a purse-size pack of Kleenex, a tube of Burt's Bees Shea Butter Hand Repair Crème, a small tin of lip balm, a comb. No sleeping pills. No pain pills. She checked the top of the counter and inside the medicine cabinet in the ensuite. No drugs. Not even over-the-counter Tylenol. *The room is as drug-free as a Christian Science church.*

Chapter 20

Dumont hated the city. The traffic was a nightmare and the noise relentless. You couldn't escape either. Massive trucks on the highway, airplanes taking off overhead, the screech of busses braking. It all grated on his nerves. Nothing, not even promotion, could get him to transfer to this place.

He wasn't keen on interviewing here, but he had to admit the Thirty-third Division cops were good guys. He'd been through basic training with two of them. Amazing how easy it was to slip back into the old, back-slapping ways. He'd go deep into his pocket for beers at the local pub this evening.

He sat in the borrowed office and looked at the woman across from him. *Not a lot of grief here.* Maybe it was shock? On the phone, she had voiced surprise rather than sorrow, but had been eager to cooperate. After all, a sister didn't get murdered every day. She understood the necessity of being here to answer questions. Of course she would help if she could.

She was attractive in a manufactured sort of way. Wavy, ice-blond hair, thin body and heavy makeup. Her face was young, her mouth wide, but her neck was surprisingly wrinkled. Did that mean she'd had a face lift? *Gina would know,* he thought. *I miss her.*

Snap to it, Dumont.

The woman was already talking. She liked to talk.

"My sister was younger by a few years, but she didn't look it,"

Andrea Mason said. She had the breathy voice of a teenager. "Everyone always thought we were twins."

Dumont sighed. So she was *that* sort of witness. It was going to be all about her. Competitive too. He braced himself.

"I think the divorce really hit her hard. Of course, her husband was a jerk, but what man isn't at that age? At least, what rich, aging man," she carefully added. "Not someone young like you." Her smile was predatory.

"I told her to not be so dramatic about it all. I mean, we're all modern, aren't we? Move with the times, I said. Have a little affair on the side if you want. But don't divorce the man just because he needs a little female reassurance."

Her fingers were drumming on her knee. "Can I smoke in here?"

Dumont shook his head.

She sighed dramatically. "Too romantic, that's what she was. Couldn't bear not to come first. I tell you, that sort of nonsense just gets you into trouble. So she divorced him. And she's been lonely ever since."

I hate her, Dumont thought suddenly. But he kept quiet and let Andrea tell all.

"It was all so predictable and banal. She started hanging around cougar bars. Just so degrading, don't you think? I mean, why not a golf instructor or personal trainer? At any rate," the fingers drummed relentlessly, "about three months ago, she called me to say she'd met this gorgeous guy. She was over the top about him. I said, 'Good for you, do you want to bring him over?'" Andrea smiled. "She didn't. I don't know if she was ashamed of him or if she didn't want to take the chance of losing him to me. But I never saw him."

Dumont sat quietly with the photo in his hand. Damnation. She wouldn't be able to recognize him.

"Do you recall his name?" Dumont said.

"She called him Reggie, I think," Andrea said. "I know he was dark, and hung like a bull—oops. Shouldn't have said that." Andrea was flirting now. "You can hardly place them up against the wall for a police line-up." Her laugh tinkled.

Dumont shifted uncomfortably in his chair.

"Is there anyone else she might have talked to about this man, Mrs. Mason?"

Andrea smoothed the black crepe skirt over her bony knees. "Can't think of anyone offhand. There were her tennis friends at the club, but I don't think they were especially close. She went to Babalon, you know—the hair salon. They might know something. But I think you can take it from me she kept this guy pretty much under wraps. Hell of a lot of competition out there, if you get my drift."

"Do you know where they would meet, Mrs. Mason?"

"Her condo by the lake, I imagine. She lived in Harbour Castle. I have a key, if you'd like it. I brought it with me." She reached into her purse and pulled out a key chain with a tag on it. "That's the suite number."

Dumont took it. "Thank you. That should make things quicker." At least this woman was intelligent.

"Oh. And of course you won't know about the cottage in Muskoka. My sister inherited that from the parents. I got the Florida condo. Have you ever been to Palm Beach, Inspector?" Her eyes belied her age.

Dumont cleared his throat. "Can you give me the address of the cottage, please?"

"Of course. I'll write it down." She took out a little gold notebook and slid the matching pen out of the slip.

As she wrote, Dumont frowned in thought. Reggie had to be somewhere. Would he be so dumb as to stay in town? The cottage was a better shot, maybe. And then he had a thought.

"Did she have a lot of good jewellery, Mrs. Mason?"

Andrea smiled. "You don't know our set very well, do you, Inspector? Her engagement ring alone was worth forty thousand and she never took it off. She had a gorgeous four-karat sapphire cocktail ring and several diamond bracelets and earrings. She got to keep them all after the divorce, of course. That's what we do, Inspector. Just like the eastern women who collect gold bangles. We have a shitload of jewellery, all our own, just in case. My European mother used to call it 'get out of town' jewellery, just in case you had to bribe your way out of the country."

Dumont looked up sharply. There had been no diamond ring on the victim's finger.

"Can you describe or draw those rings?"

"Of course," she said, drawing on the small pad. "The diamond is pear shaped—like this—and about 10 karats. From Birks, so it's a good one. The sapphire is a marquis with diamonds all around it. She also had two-karat diamond solitaire earrings and a bunch of others. Her newest watch was a Piaget. You should find a record of all this in her files in the second bedroom. Look under *Jewellery*."

Dumont had to ask. "How do you know where to look in her files?"

Andrea blinked. "But Inspector, we always keep records. It's only logical. Mom taught us well."

He managed to be somewhat polite as he escorted her out of the office and declined her invitation for lunch at the Bloor Street Diner.

Yes, he would be in touch if he needed anything more. *Good God.*

He went back to the office and phoned his staff. "Jackson, get down here. I need you to check out all the pawnshops in the city. Here's what I want you to do..."

Five minutes later he leaned back in the chair. First the condo and then the cottage in Muskoka.

Gord sat at the desk in the study and scowled at the papers in front of him. "I became a doctor so I wouldn't have to deal with all this financial crap. Let the accountants and lawyers do it."

Tony smiled. "It's pretty much in order, from what I can tell. When the investments are sold off, Gina should have a little over two million. We split the bulk of the estate three ways: between Gina, Ian and myself. Nellie gets the house and a million bucks, and Becki gets a smaller, specified amount."

Gord looked up in surprise. "That much? I wouldn't have imagined. Where did it come from? Her old man was frugal, but not that big an earner."

"Inherited from a cousin in the old country. Some apartments were sold. I handled the transactions from this end."

Gord removed his reading glasses. He was a tall, trim man with receding grey hair. Despite what Gord said about not wanting to deal with financial crap, Tony thought his uncle was perhaps the most intelligent man he had ever met. There was a lot going on behind those hazel eyes.

"I have two things on my mind," Gord said in his even baritone. "I know about you and Gina. It was the first thing out of her mouth when we arrived. Not that we hadn't been expecting something of the kind. Or at least, Anna had."

Tony shifted in his chair. God, he was uncomfortable. What was he supposed to do or say?

"I've only one thing to say about that. Treat her well, Tony. She's the most valuable thing in my life."

Tony leaned forward. He felt better; these were words he could relate to. "I feel the same, sir."

Gord looked at him, appraising, and then nodded once. "Now, tell me what the hell has been going on around here."

Dumont stood in the hallway of suite 2628 and looked around. He almost whistled. The view out the floor to ceiling windows was breathtaking. Sunlight bounced off the water. He could see the lake glistening with the Toronto islands smack ahead. Little toy boats peppered the harbour, although he reflected they probably wouldn't appear so little when seen close up. Yup, this was a million-dollar view and likely to cost at least that much.

"Not too shabby, eh?" Janet Mitchem said beside him. She was a newly-made sergeant, bright and dependable.

"Over my budget," Dumont replied. "I'll take the master. You look for the files."

The condo was one of those lofty, two-story jobs, with two bedrooms upstairs and main living quarters downstairs. Dumont took the half set of stairs to his right; Janet followed. The two bedrooms had the same view as downstairs. He went to the bigger one first, the one with the en-suite bathroom.

It was definitely a woman's room, done up in creams and caramels. The satiny bed was made up and there weren't any clothes hanging on chairs or floors. Not like his apartment. This lady was neat.

Dumont went to the long dresser, and sure enough there was a big jewellery box, front and centre. Every woman had one, in his experience. He pulled the little tiny pulls. The drawers opened. Nothing. Huh? It was empty. All those little compartments. Well, well.

He started opening dresser drawers. One had just silk scarves in it, no jeweller's boxes. Imagine...a whole drawer with nothing but scarves. The next had panties. That's all. The next, bras. He scooted through the middle and bottom drawers. No sign of any jewellery. The place had been cleaned out.

He could hear Janet opening drawers in the next room.

"Janet, come here," he said.

Her face framed by the brown helmet of hair appeared in the doorway.

"Take a peek at this, and tell me if you can think of any other place the vic might have put her jewellery."

Janet looked at the empty jewellery box. She opened the scarf drawer and then looked at him. "I'll check the walk-in, but this shouldn't be empty. And I'll check the freezer in the fridge, just in case she was planning to go away. But I think someone's cleaned her out. Could it be the sister?"

Dumont thought, then shook his head. "Don't think so. She wouldn't have been so forthcoming about giving me descriptions."

"Speaking of which..." Janet left the room for a second and came back. "I found the appraisals for her jewellery. She had lots, all right. And you should see the value."

Dumont frowned. It was hard to hock a lot of jewellery in this town, but if you weren't too fussy where you went...Damn. He could be all the way to Egypt right now. Or Eastern Europe, or South America. Dumont's cop sense told him they were never going to see Reggie again.

He couldn't have been more wrong.

Chapter 21

Nellie gathered around her the things she needed to be a spy. Or a detective. Or one of the kids from her book, *The Island of Adventure*. Those kids solved a puzzle together so she could too. But it had to be all by herself. Not with the help of a brother or sister because she didn't have one. And not with Abigail because this was the real-life mystery of whether it was Father who killed that lady outside their house. Everyone said Father put Mom in the hospital and Nellie believed it. And that was bad enough.

Did he murder his friend too? The one who laughed and giggled with him and snuck into her room with him that night when they thought she was asleep.

Nellie bet Mom still didn't know about that. Mom was in the hospital then too. Not because Father hit her, but because she was depressed or something and needed rest.

Her stuff was strewn all around her as she sat on the floor of her bedroom. So far she'd collected a hand mirror, a magnifying glass, a flashlight, binoculars, paper, a pencil, a tape recorder, an old knapsack to carry everything in and a knife to protect herself.

Mission number one was to check Father and Mom's room. Father was gone since sometime yesterday. So it wasn't like he'd be there taking a nap or anything. She scrabbled to her door, opened it, poked the mirror around the door frame and angled it so she could see down the hall. No one. And no one was coming up the stairs either. Then she angled it up the hall. She hadn't heard any noises coming from any of the bedrooms in a long time so that meant everyone was downstairs. *The coast is clear.*

She crawled back to her pile of equipment, stashed it in her knapsack, pulled it over her shoulders, stood up and tip-toed to the door. This time she peeked with her eyes. Still completely safe.

Mom and Father's room was right next door. So she didn't have to go far. She opened their door and slipped inside.

She wiped her hand across her forehead. *No one saw.* But her heart was pounding for real. She wasn't supposed to be in their bedroom when she wasn't invited. Funny, because she was allowed to go everywhere else in the house. Oh ya, but not in guest rooms when people were staying over.

Her stomach growled. This adventure was making her starving. She'd have to remember to pack cookies or something next time.

First thing she decided to check was whether Father took his overnight bag or his suitcase with him. That would let her know how long he was going to be away. Whenever he was about to leave on a business trip to Toronto, either the small, black overnight bag would be sitting by the front door, or the really big one with the handle and wheels that pulled out. She headed for their closet because she knew he stored them in there when he wasn't using them. He let her watch him pack and unpack sometimes. She opened the double doors and pushed past a bunch of his suits. She discovered that both his overnight bag *and* his suitcase were missing.

Next she checked his dresser. No big pile of socks in his sock drawer. She didn't know whether to be happy or sad that he was going to be gone for a long, long time.

She knew from bits of movies and TV shows she should search for blood to know for absolute sure if he did it. She got down on her hands and knees and searched every crook and cranny, including the whole en-suite, for a sign of blood. Nothing. Now she could go back to her room and tell Macho that Father was not a murderer. But she wanted to do one more thing. She took out her pencil and rubbed the lead gently back and forth over the scratch pad by the phone. Even the kids at school knew if you rubbed gently, whatever message was last written on the pad would show up white.

"Carla, did you sort through your mom's stuff already?" Becki was still wondering how there could be no drugs at all.

"What do you mean?"

"In her room?"

"I thought Anna said she wanted to do that."

"And I wanted to help. I was planning to dispose of Godmom's pharmaceuticals and I couldn't find them. Just thought it was weird."

"Oh, I see. That's right. I cleaned out her drugs. Nellie has the run of the place, and I didn't want her coming across something dangerous."

"Smart."

"And while I was doing that, I found and picked out Mom's diamond watch from inside her nightstand. She left it to you, right? I put it in my room so I'd remember to give it to you, but...well...other things sort of happened. I didn't get around to it. Sorry. But now I'm thinking about it, I'll go get it."

"Carla, you're wearing a cast."

"So?"

"You shouldn't be going up and down stairs. In fact, you should move down here until your cast comes off. If we finish cleaning out your mom's room, would you consider using it?"

"No."

"Not even temporarily?"

"No." Carla moved away.

"At least don't worry about that watch. I'm in no hurry to have it."

"It's beautiful," said Carla over her shoulder.

"The watch she wore every day?"

"No, the Piaget was her dress-up watch. And she kept it in its original case. Let me go get it."

"Carla!"

"What? Have to keep moving."

Carla didn't want to give Mom's beautiful watch to Becki. After all, Becki wasn't family. So even if she hadn't been that annoying lately, and stayed by her side at the hospital, and went with her to the police station, and bought Nellie that book, and didn't seem to be judging her for marrying Reggie in the first place, it felt wrong. She climbed the stairs slowly. Awkwardly. Horribly wrong. She walked up the hall to her bedroom like Frankenstein with a club foot.

Chapter 22

"Come take a walk with me," her dad said after dinner.

Gina smiled as she rose. 'Dark walks' with her dad had been a nightly tradition all through her late childhood and teen years. She still loved the night air, the quiet and the feeling of safety that Dad brought to the night.

They walked side by side in silence until they reached the town sidewalk.

"I spoke with Tony," Gord said finally. "About this whole mess and about you."

Gina let out her breath.

"Tell me you didn't say some nonsense about being honourable, Dad." Good grief, how embarrassing that would be.

"Didn't have to," Gord said. The smile was in his voice. "You better love that fellow, Gina, because I don't think he's going to accept no for an answer."

Now Gina felt silly. She didn't know what to say.

"Do you love him, sweetheart? I've got to hear you say it. It's just the two of us here so you can be honest."

It came easy now, the words and the confidence that went with them. "Yes. Yes I do, Dad. I think I always have."

"That's what your mom said." Her dad sounded satisfied.

They walked on. The small sounds of night in this town were sweetly calming, unlike the relentless noise of the city.

"For what it's worth, I think he's a good man, Gina. He was a good kid; I liked him even then. I'd be proud to have him in the family—yes, you can giggle about that, considering. But it's up to you, sweetheart. You know that."

She knew. That was the great thing about Dad. He was always there to support you. Always there, period. A hard act for anyone to follow.

"Do you think it's Reggie?"

Gina nearly tripped on the sidewalk. "What?"

"Everyone is saying Reggie is the murderer. Do you think so?"

She stopped walking, turned to her dad and said, "No."

"I don't, either." Gord searched her face. "Do you know who it is?"

Gina hesitated, then remembered who she was talking to. "I have an idea. But I don't have any proof and no one will believe it."

"How sure are you?" Gord said.

Gina licked her lips. "Not sure at all." How to explain, the philosophy she had been playing with. That the whole world came down to a few things that were all-important. And all you had to do was look at what was most important to each person...

"Could you be in danger?"

Gina shook her head. "I'm not a threat. And no one would guess what I'm thinking."

Gord reached over to wrap his arm about her. "Keep it to yourself, sweetheart. Don't tell a soul, not even Tony. Don't even hint about it. I'm not sure we're done with it all yet."

Gina felt a chill to her toes. It wasn't over—she knew that too.

Linda was holding court in the kitchen when they got back.

"All I said was they let the bastard get away."

"They don't know for sure it was Reggie," Becki said sensibly.

"Oh, don't be ridiculous. Who else could it be? Reggie was screwing that blond slut and he got tired of her. She tried to make things difficult for him...was going to tell Carla or something. Don't tell me it was the first time. That type is always prowling."

"Linda, keep your voice down. Carla might hear. She's only in the bathroom." The disgust in Mandy's voice was clear.

"You think she doesn't know? Carla's no dummy. She's well rid of him, if you ask me. We all are. I'm just surprised she didn't do him in herself. Now there's the person who should have died."

"Maybe she did." Ian spoke from the side.

"What are you talking about?"

"Sweetie, that's brilliant," Linda said.

"I don't understand." Gina heard her mom's voice from the corner.

"Reggie's missing. Maybe he didn't run away. Maybe Carla offed him and packed his stuff to make it look like he ran off."

"Linda!" Becki exclaimed. "That's a terrible thing to say."

"What? You think Carla couldn't kill anyone? She could do it well enough if given the right reason. So could I."

Gord stood in the doorway, leaning against the jam. "A regular Lady Macbeth you are, Linda."

"Really?" Linda looked over and drawled, "I always imagined myself as Cleopatra."

"Why not?" Mandy muttered. "They both used poison."

When Gina woke up the first time, the moon was still high. When she woke up the second time, it had hardly moved. She tossed and turned for a while and finally gave up.

Her dressing gown was draped across the end of the bed. She donned it. The hall was cold and empty; moonlight drifted in from the staircase window. She moved to the landing. At the bottom of the stairs was the kitchen with its comfort of tea. She hesitated and then turned the other way. She took each step softly, slowly, to the third floor.

What was she doing? Was she mad? At the door to his room, she peeked in. In the dark, she could find no one there. Where was he? The loss hit her like a blow to the chest.

Then he was behind her, wordlessly taking her arm, pulling her into the room and the door shut behind them.

The sun was fully up when Gina woke next.

They were in Tony's room at the back of the house. It had always been his room in the old days and she had envied him for it...the sloped ceiling, the low, gabled windows. The place had been full of comic books and matchbox cars. Of course, girls weren't allowed in the attic room then.

There was no one else on the third floor, which made it private.

Gina revelled in the glorious aftermath of being made love to in a dozen different ways. Tony was on his back. Her head snuggled against the side of his chest. *My God, my God, could anything feel so good ever again?* she wondered. The steady sound of his breathing, of his chest rising and falling made a soothing rhythm. She was almost asleep again when the soft pounding started.

"Gina, Gina. Are you in there?" It was only a whisper, but Gina bolted right up. *Caught. Oh my goodness, what to do?*

"It's Becki. Look, Tony, is Gina in there with you? Everyone's looking for her."

Tony was awake now. He was smiling and his eyes twinkled.

"Tell them to stop," he said. "Squirt is safe enough."

Gina stared at him in horror and then picked up a pillow and whacked him with it.

"Ouch!" Tony yelped. "But I might need help."

Gina could almost hear the smile in Becki's voice. "Get up, you two. I'll try to keep people off the second floor so you can go down and get dressed, Gina. Make it snappy."

Gina moved to lunge off the bed, but Tony caught her arm.

"Hey, not so fast." He pulled her down on top of him.

"Tony, no! I've got to—" But it appeared she didn't have to, after all.

Chapter 23

"Macho, you know what? Mom nearly caught me yesterday when I was searching her room." She hated it when Mom was upset with her.

Macho raised his head.

"Lucky I hid in the closet."

He slumped in relief.

"Didn't think she'd be as mad as Father, so I almost came out and let her know I was there." She frowned. "But Mom limped across the room to her nightstand, took this sparkly bracelet thing out, sat down, put it around her wrist and then started crying. Ya, crying. Father wasn't even there to yell at her or hit her, and she started crying anyway. All by herself. And I felt really sorry for her and thought I should comfort her like when she comforts me when I'm sad."

She hugged Macho to show him how she wanted to hug Mom.

"But I didn't, 'cause I wasn't sure, and she left, and I don't think she even knew I was there."

Nellie looked around her bedroom. Sun streamed in the window and in its path, she could see dust floating down like snowflakes. All those slanted rays of sunlight also highlighted her knapsack in a heap on the floor on the other side of the room. She crawled over to it.

"You know what else?" Not waiting for Macho to answer, she pulled the tape recorder from her bag. "Last night I caught Uncle Jerry and Aunt Linda having a fight on tape. I heard them arguing through their door, couldn't hear exactly what they were saying, so I stuck this microphone under it." She held up a tiny black mic on a wire that was plugged into her machine. "Wanna hear?"

She pressed *Rewind* and the tape spun backward with a whirring sound. Then she pressed *Play*.

"And for God's sake, Linda, instead of wasting thousands of dollars on creams and potions, why don't you bloody quit smoking?"

"None of your business, Jerry."

"None of my business?"

"What I do doesn't concern you."

"What you do affects me. We're married."

"Right."

"For instance, I married a beautiful, young woman, who'll very soon be a wrinkled, old hag, despite the fact she spends thousands of dollars, not to mention thousands of hours, fighting destructive—"

"Finished yet?"

"Well, no, actually. Let me add that beautiful, young woman I married will end up prematurely dead from lung cancer and I have to watch it happen. Linda Ferrero's suicide drama in slow motion."

"Like you care. And as if you don't have your own vices that are just as hateful to me."

"Turn it around, why don't you?"

"Like you're the injured party—Mr. Tom Cat."

"What?"

"You heard me. Youth and beauty are all you care about. Why do you think you fell for me in the first place? And now that I'm older, you're on to greener pastures. Greener. Sexier. As in secretary? As in poor, lonely divorcée? Why be picky? As long as they have looks. I should say, as long as they have gravity-defying boobs."

"Go ahead and kill yourself with cigarettes."

"Maybe you'd like to speed things up. Is that what happened to Hilary?"

"Hilary?"

"Got too long in the tooth for you?"

"What you talking about?"

"That woman! That woman in red. She one of yours? You kill her?"

"Are you crazy? First you accuse Carla of killing. And now me? You're too much, Linda. Way too much. I'm not listening to another word. I'm asleep. Sound asleep in my bed."

"Fine!"

"Snore."

The tape went silent. Nellie pressed *Stop*. She rubbed her hand over her forehead—her fingers fluttered. "I should probably tell Mom, right?"

"Mom, I think Tony's carrying a gun," Becki said.

What makes you say that?

"Caught a glimpse of something that looks like Karl's bulge when he's carrying."

Looking at other men's bulges?

"You never used to be like this, Mom."

Never used to be dead.

"Will you be serious? There's been a murder and I think someone I know is carrying a weapon."

Your husband's the cop. Not you. What're you doing snooping around? You'll get yourself in big doo doo like this.

"I'm not snooping. Just happened to notice. What do you think it means?"

The woman who died wasn't shot, was she?

"No, she was beaten with a bat."

Tony wearing a bat too?

"For God's sake, Mom."

Call your husband. That's my advice. You're missing him. That's what this is.

"For once I think you're right."

Becki dialled home.

"Hi, Karl."

"Hi, honey. How's it going?"

"Okay. You?"

"I'm good."

"Haven't gained more weight, have you?"

"Maintaining. Are you free to come home?"

"Not yet."

"Oh."

"In the meantime, I have a question for you."

"Hit me."

"Wish I could."

"Huh?"

"Wish I could touch you."

"Me too. Ah, your question. Go ahead."

"What would you say if I told you Tony's wearing a gun? But it's hidden. Is that legal?"

"Hmmm. A concealed weapon. In Canada. Only cops and criminals carry guns."

"Which category do architects fall under?"

"Maybe you should stay away from him while I do a little research."

"Weird. We've known Tony for years."

"And don't rile him up."

"Hey, I never rile people up. Especially Tony. He seems like such a nice guy."

"Still, don't let him know you're on to him. I said cops *and* criminals."

The loneliness hit her again as soon as she hung up the phone.

Chapter 24

"Air Canada says no passenger of that name traveled with them in the past week. Checking WestJet now. But you know, Guv, if the suspect went stateside, he could hop a flight from Buffalo and we'd never know. That's what I would do."

Rob scowled into the phone. And it was so easy to slip from there into Mexico and then further south, if you wanted. Who knows where the man had connections…Right. He had some follow-up to do.

"Thanks, Janet. I'm on my way back to the house to question the wife."

Rob drove above the speed limit without noticing. This was the part of the investigation that got tedious. Parcel out a bunch of leads…check every one of them out…wait for the results to come back in. Ninety-nine out of a hundred led nowhere, or sometimes they led to ten more avenues of investigation which themselves led to more…

But this was what being a good cop was all about. The painstaking details. The ferreting…the relentless asking of questions and sorting through facts. Eliminating the extraneous and salvaging the few leads that could go somewhere.

Rob was good at that. He had a true cop's gut and he knew he was on to something now.

Carla didn't look good, Rob had to admit. The skin around her eyes had gone from black to purple and green, and she made no attempt to hide the bruising with makeup. Her mouth was still a mess. It hurt to look at her.

Besides that, she was sullen. Perhaps it hurt to smile?

"Have you found the bastard?" She spit the words.

Whoa. Guess that established how she was feeling. Rob squirmed in the study chair.

"Not yet, but we have some leads. Perhaps you can help us."

Carla merely stared at the floor.

"We think he might have left the country. Perhaps Mexico or further south. Did he have any connections there that you can think of? Any foreign connections he could stay with?"

Now she looked up, startled. "In Mexico? How the devil would he get there?"

Rob shifted uneasily. "We're checking flights now."

Carla merely laughed. "Well you can stop that right away. Reggie would never fly. Don't you know? He was terrified of planes. He couldn't even go up a stepladder without fainting or throwing up."

Rob frowned. "It would have been useful if you'd told us this before."

Now she sneered at him. "It would be useful if you could do your job and find the bastard who did this to me. So don't lecture me."

Rob felt his face go red and his blood pressure mount. *Steady now*—he was losing his cool. He turned back to face her. "Mrs. Williamson. If you know of any place your husband could be or anyone he could be staying with, please tell me now."

Carla looked away. Her whole body seemed to fold into a hunch.

"Nowhere you have to fly to. Reggie liked trains. He used to say you met the most interesting people on trains. Mainly older women with money, I expect. He seemed to know a lot of those." Her voice sounded defeated.

"He could take a train to the States and then across the border south," Rob suggested.

She shrugged. It looked like it hurt to do that. "Could have. But he never mentioned ever wanting to go there. We went to Vegas once, but that was about it. Didn't meet anyone there to speak of."

"What about friends? Did he have any male friends?"

Carla shook her head. "Men didn't like him."

Rob sighed deeply. This was like pulling teeth.

"So you can't think of anywhere he might have gone to? Anyone who might be giving him shelter?"

"What an odd way to put it. 'Anyone who might give him shelter,' like he was a dog or something. That's it! That's what he was—a hound dog." She laughed and the sound verged on hysteria.

Rob stared. He had known Carla since he was a kid, and while he'd never warmed to her, it bothered him to see her this way.

"Oh, Lord," she said, huffing for air. "I can see some old bitch putting him in the dog house, patting him down for the night." And then she was off again, cackling like a Halloween witch.

"You can go now. Send Gina in if you see her," Rob said, waving her away. "But if you think of anything—"

"I know." She gasped for breath. "I'll call you."

Watching her rise from the chair was painful. She moved slowly to the door and then turned. "If I were you, I'd look in some place like Palm Beach. Those wealthy Toronto matrons go to Florida every year, don't they?" With that, she left.

Rob looked down at the desk, deep in thought.

A minute later, Gina walked in.

"Good morning, Rob. You wanted to see me?"

His eyes lit up immediately and he jumped to his feet.

"Come in. Sit down. Have you had coffee yet?"

Gina's smile was perky. "Actually, it's my house, of a sort. I should be asking you that."

Rob blushed and sat. "Sorry. Foolish of me." He ran his eyes over her. She looked lovely in that deep blue sweater and blue jeans. The blue did something to her skin—something nice.

"I just need you to confirm some things. I need the opinion of someone I know and trust."

He looked directly at her. Gina nodded.

"Mrs. Williamson tells me her husband was afraid of flying."

Gina nodded again. "It's true. We all knew that. I think it was fear of heights rather than air sickness."

Rob leaned back. "So he wouldn't have taken a plane anywhere, in your opinion."

She shook her head. "Never. I can't swear to it but—no, I just don't believe he could make himself get on one."

"That narrows the search a bit." Rob chewed on the end of a pen. "Can you think of any place he would go? Or someone who would harbour him?"

She crossed her legs and linked hands around her knees. "You are thinking he has a woman in every port, maybe. I'm not sure about that. I would put him down as a serial monogamist. You know, the type who needs the fix of falling in love, of being adored and then tires of the person after a while. Or perhaps more likely they stop adoring him when they find out his true nature, and he's compelled to move on. But I don't see him with several women at one time."

Rob continued to chew thoughtfully. "Interesting. So you're saying women start out loving him and then are disappointed?"

"I would think that is a likely pattern. You know he has been married before. Why don't you follow this up with his first wife?"

Damn and blast. Always, Gina had good ideas. "I'll do that," Rob said. Then he decided to be brave. "Gina, I kind of messed things up with Tony. I don't know if he mentioned it."

"Don't worry about it," she said quickly. "Leave Tony to me."

Rob stared at her. There was something about her—some new confidence making him uneasy. Why was she blushing like that?

A guitar riff startled them both.

Rob picked up the phone. "Whacha got for me?"

"Kilkenny's pawn on Sherbourne. Got a ring matching one of the descriptions, and a few other things of interest."

"Lock the place up. On my way."

Rob shut off the phone. "Sorry, Gina. Gotta go."

He felt that old surge of adrenalin rise within him. Within seconds, he was out the door.

Chapter 25

On his way to the pawn shop, Rob reviewed a piece of physical evidence in the case—the murder weapon. It might have been languishing under the overhang, against the back wall of the Ferrero garage before it was wielded to kill Hilary Best. Jerry said he, Giuseppe, Anna and Carla never played softball as kids, but he did remember playing pick-up games as an adult with his brother and their two sons, Ian and Tony, and some of the other neighbourhood kids. *Including me,* thought Rob—*on weekends and holidays when families in Langdon Hills gathered to celebrate.*

Trouble with that was it meant the entire Ferrero family, friends and neighbours could have recalled where the game bat was stashed. Some of whom—Jerry, Gina, Tony, Mandy and Becki, for instance—were willing to go so far as to state the bat *looked familiar*. But hell, if it was that same old bat, any stranger off the street could have grabbed it.

Rob did have several hard facts about the weapon. Like the brand—Louisville Slugger. The model—400SB. And maybe a serial number painted on the wood with black paint—80-2110-4.

He'd studied the company website on the Internet and used the Dealer Locator function to discover Louisville Sluggers were only available in the States. He'd put a call through to their consumer inquiry line to see if they could offer up any information as to manufacture date, purchase date, retailer, purchaser…Nothing.

Of course, the bat handle had prints. It was smeared by more than a decade's worth of big-game-organizing fingers. A health hazard long before it met with Hilary's skull. He hoped Kilkenny's proved more instructive.

Becki thought it was a shame about gay guys. She didn't disapprove of their lifestyle—no, lifestyle was the wrong word because it indicated some kind of choice and she didn't think they had one—but women lost out when a good-looking, kind, sensitive, talented, fun guy played for the other team. Ian being the exception to the rule because he exhibited so few of those qualities. Okay, maybe in a pinch she'd give him talented. Which was what she was thinking when she sat down on the long chair next to Ian's chaise on the back deck. "How's it going?" she asked.

"Like crap," he said.

"Messed up right now," she agreed. She leaned back and eased her feet up onto the seat cushion.

"Taking off tomorrow. Don't care if they haven't found Reggie. Don't care if they don't know for sure it was him who killed that woman. I'm leaving. They can come arrest me in Toronto if they want me that bad. *Design at Nine* can't afford to hold off production one more day. And Andrew...Well, Andrew's another story altogether."

"Hmmm," said Becki. "Nice day, eh?"

"Swell."

"Warm for September, even. Can't remember the last time it was nice like this...I'm going to get a cold drink. Want one?"

Ian rolled, turning his back.

"Ian?" she asked.

He waved his arm dismissively.

She planted her feet firmly on the deck. Walked to the back door and stepped into the kitchen. A maple leaf swirled through with her on a breeze from outside. The screen slapped her back. She took off her shoes and walked across the black and white tiles. She'd barely opened the fridge when there was a crack.

"What was that?" she exclaimed to no one in particular because there was no one else in the kitchen, but it was an automatic reaction, kind of like tripping on the sidewalk and turning to look at the spot that tripped you.

A car backfiring? No, the noise came from the back of the house, not the street. And it was close.

She shut the fridge door and listened. Nothing more. But it wasn't her imagination. The crack was real. Sill...no reason to go all haywire. She dismissed what was probably the least likely explanation, yet it shoved its way back to the front of her thoughts anyway. Because of

Hilary Best.

No, it had to be some poor squirrel blasted to kingdom come off a Langdon Hills Hydro transformer. It happened. Once in Black Currant Bay, a grey squirrel shorted out the town's electricity for an entire long weekend.

She opened the fridge door again. Checking. The interior light was working. Without taking a beverage, she marched back to her shoes, put them on, pushed open the screen door, stepped out, took one deep breath and surveyed the back lawn from the far left. No wires where a squirrel might have met his maker. Ahead in the distance, past the maple tree, she saw the bench Mandy had been sitting on that morning, the spot where Hilary Best was found, and the pathway where she herself discovered Carla wandering in a daze. No fallen branches to explain the loud crack. Nothing out of the ordinary. It was when she scanned to her right that she saw Ian, nearly falling off his lounger, one arm trailing the boards of the deck, and a stain like a target on his back.

She screamed. Or not. Pins of light darted in front of her eyes like a test for peripheral vision. *Secure the scene? Check for a pulse? Call an ambulance?* She thought she remembered *secure the scene* was the first step in an emergency. It was crucial to do something.

Chapter 26

Gina was breathless.

Tony pulled Becki away from the body. "Stay back, Gina. Don't come any closer."

"Is it...?"

"Ian. He's dead. Get Becki out of here. Don't leave her side and don't let her talk. No, wait." He dug in his pocket and came out with a cellphone. "Call Rob first. It's on speed-dial. Make sure you get through to him. Tell him I'm securing the scene."

Gina nodded. She seemed to be walking through a stage play. Nothing seemed real. Here was Becki sobbing quietly, while Ian wasn't making a sound. It wasn't like Ian at all to be silent at a time like this. Ian relished drama. But then, nothing would ever be like Ian again. *Oh, Lord.*

"Wait a minute," said Tony. "Where's Linda?"

"At the hair salon with your mom."

"And Jerry?"

"I don't know. In town somewhere waiting for them."

"Your parents?"

"Shopping."

"Take her in to the kitchen, and give her some tea. Don't let anyone out here, Gina."

Becki was stiff to the touch. Gina took her gently by the shoulders and steered her into the kitchen.

Tony stood over the body, frowning. Made to look like suicide, for sure. But Ian wasn't the type to end it, and if he were, it wouldn't be this way. There would be a dramatic scene before and a full audience. He would have left numerous farewell letters and elaborate instructions for the funeral.

Tony looked around. No notes, of course. Just a whole lot of blood.

The gun was a 9 mil. He'd never seen it before, as far as he knew. He wouldn't touch it, of course. Wonder who it was registered to? If it was registered.

No, this was murder, he was sure of it. And it made him so angry he could hardly keep from hitting the brick wall with his fist.

Twenty minutes later, Rob stood looking over the body. "Why the hell don't they do it in the bathtub?"

"What are you talking about?" Tony muttered.

"Suicides. You wouldn't believe how many of them do it on the living room floor. Impossible to clean up after. Bloody selfish, if you ask me. At least you'll be able to wash down the deck here."

Tony looked at Rob and frowned. "This wasn't suicide."

Rob walked around the side of the body. "You sure? Gun's in the right place."

Tony shook his head. "Suicides don't shoot themselves through the heart. They blow their brains out. And the psychology is all wrong. You know Ian. He'd want television cameras and a brass band."

Rob looked up. "That's harsh."

Tony cursed. "I'm so angry I can hardly breathe. I know Ian. He would never kill himself. He loved life too much, with all its scenes and drama. And after inheriting two million? It doesn't make any sense."

"Tell me more," Rob said. "Why would he be a target?"

Tony leaned back against the brick wall and crossed his arms. "As I said—I know Ian. He was a sneaky bastard. Liked to insinuate things. If he knew something about the murder, he might just hint to the murderer in his sly way. That is exactly what he might have done. Totally in character. Stupid bastard. Bloody stupid bastard." Tony heard his voice catch.

The Scenes of Crime Operatives team had arrived and came around the side of the house.

"Becki found him?"

Tony nodded. "She's in the kitchen with Gina. I told her to say nothing to anyone."

"Thanks. I'll take her in the study. You can stay with Gina in the kitchen. If any others come in, keep them there."

Tony nodded. After a perfect night, what a hell of a way to end the day.

Gina made a fresh pot of tea. She looked at the wall clock. Where was Carla? Nellie would be coming home from school soon.

Outside, the SOCO team was finishing up.

Becki was in the study with Rob now, and she had Tony to herself.

Gina looked across the kitchen table at him and wondered if she would ever be the same again. Was it only hours ago she had been lying naked in his arms? Now she could hardly look at him without having a kaleidoscope of feelings welling up inside her. She wanted to be in his arms again, but for a different reason. Ian was dead, and she wanted her older cousin close to her, comforting her.

She watched Tony's eyes focus on the screen door, deep in thought.

"I know you think Ian knew something about the first murder. But have you thought about other motives?" She handed Tony a mug of tea.

"What do you mean?"

Gina pursed her lips. She'd been thinking hard, trying to keep her mind off the fact Ian was outside, not breathing anymore. So she'd forced herself to be business-like. It was easier.

"Money. I always think money is the strongest motive, don't you? What does this mean for the will?" she said. "Ian inherited two million dollars. What happens to that money now?"

Tony looked up, alert. "I don't know. Depends on how the will is written. I can't remember the exact details."

"What do you mean?"

Tony frowned. "It might go to the person he has designated in his will. If Ian had one. Remember, he was superstitious. But it also might come to you and me. There's often a clause in a will stating the recipient must survive the dead person by thirty days."

Gina felt a chill run through her.

"But that's terrible. That leaves so many suspects."

Tony raised one eyebrow. "Explain."

She blew on her tea to cool it. "Linda and Jerry would probably think the money would come to them. I know—it's crazy to think anyone might suspect Linda of killing her own son for money, but you know what the media are like. Oh my God, the media, Tony. Ian has that cable show. We'll get reporters up here for sure."

Tony cursed. "I'd better warn Rob. He'll need to secure the place." He started to rise.

"Hold on a sec—before you do, let me think this through with you."

Gina started to panic. She didn't want to be alone in the kitchen, not with a killer about. She inhaled deeply and tried to calm herself. "Linda and Jerry are suspects, but Ian might have left everything to Andrew. Linda wouldn't think of that." She took a sip from her mug. Her right hand shook, so she braced the mug with the left. "Did you ever meet Andrew?"

Tony shook his head.

"I have several times," Gina said. "And I know things were rocky between Ian and Andrew. Andrew is quite good-looking and younger. He was sleeping around a bit—no, don't interrupt me. I know what I'm talking about. It was common gossip at the studio. Now, look," she leaned forward, "if Andrew thought he might inherit the two million that makes him a suspect too."

Tony nodded. He watched Gina closely. "Andrew knows Ian is going to change his will, that's what you're saying. So he strikes now, while Reg is still a suspect for the first murder. Nice piece of camouflage...burying one murder within another. Different motive...different killer. And the first one gets blamed."

Gina nodded. "And Tony—you're saying the full eight million, after the legacies, might be split between you and me now since Ian is dead. That makes us suspects. Actually, even our parents could be suspects for the same reason."

He scowled. "That's crazy. No one would suspect you. You just inherited two million—who the hell cares about more? Nobody would kill for that."

"Ah, but you forget. I identified the first victim, Tony. As far as the police know, I was one of the few people who knew Hilary Best. I didn't really know her, of course, but I knew who she was. There was a connection. You can bet the police have got my photo up there on the suspect board."

Tony stared. She could practically see his mind clicking over as he processed this new angle. "How long have you been worried about this?"

Gina raised the mug to her lips and took a long sip. After a pause, she said, "Since last night. It didn't register at first, since I was so darn proud of making the identification. Then it slowly dawned on me that maybe I hadn't been too smart about it from my own point of view."

Tony shook his head. "Rob doesn't suspect you."

"Don't discount this, Tony. We'll be treated as suspects. That's the hell of it."

"What? Say it."

Gina cleared her throat. "It hardly matters who actually inherits. What matters is who thought they might."

Chapter 27

Rob paced the floor. *Shut this bloody rampage down, Dumont.*

Serial murder just didn't happen in Langdon Hills. Had any murder ever occurred here before? Certainly not since his debut in law enforcement. And before that he'd lived his whole childhood in this town and try as he might, he couldn't remember a single murder. Not even way back when in his parents' or grandparents' day.

Things were so close to veering out of control. He could see that. But no, he wasn't going to ask for help. He was still in charge and wasn't going to blow this unique opportunity to use all his training, and prove himself. Above and beyond. But if the investigation went on much longer, he'd have to appeal to the OPP, or the RCMP, or both. No choice.

Speaking of the feds, Secret Agent Man was on site. Rob didn't know exactly what the deal was with Tony's gig, but if he didn't hate him quite so much, he would ask him to consult. *Stop. Hate is too strong a word.*

He and Tony Ferrero were close once. No, they used to hang together, that's all. The one year age difference gave Rob the upper hand back then. But Tony left town then dared to come back thinking he's *the man.* Dammit if Tony didn't somehow end up with Gina too. Gina and Tony were cousins, for crying out loud. Off limits. And since they only just found out they weren't blood-related, how in hell did they get moonfaced over each other so quickly?

Slow it down, Dumont. Pump it way down. Time to interview Becki, right in front of you. She's had ample opportunity to gather her thoughts.

"Now tell me everything," he said. "Everything down to the last detail. What you saw, what you heard, what you smelled, for crissake."

Detective Dumont was Becki's turn-to guy in Langdon Hills. He helped them all get through the horrible first murder that took place on the property. He was the one she contacted when she found Carla. But today he was off. Not like she remembered. And not as compassionate as he'd shown himself to be over the past several days. His pacing unnerved her. But face it, dust falling unnerved her. Maybe it was she, after all, and not he, who'd changed, since once you've discovered a second murder victim at the house you're visiting, things get hairy, right? Especially when one of the victims is someone you've known for years and years. Becki would have liked to state *known and loved for years and years.*

Rob barked his request again. "What do you remember?"

"Okay, so I came in to get something to drink..." Her thoughts felt jumbled like the letters in her morning Alpha-Bits.

"Ian was fine when you left him on the deck?"

Totally freezing in here or her imagination?

"Yes or no?"

"Yes."

"You didn't see a gun?"

"No." She thought of the gun Tony had on him the other day. Should she say something about it? *No.* Later, she'd get to it later. Or Rob would, in his interrogation.

"Keep going."

"I took off my shoes and walked to the fridge. That's when I heard the gun shot...I guess."

"You guess?"

"Well, then I thought it was a car backfiring. Or a tree branch breaking." She wasn't going to get into the whole squirrel thing.

"What did you do?"

"Went outside to check."

"Serious enough to check, then."

"Maybe in the back of my mind—"

"How long were you in the kitchen?"

"Four to five minutes."

"Who was with you inside?"

"No one."

"Sure?"

"That I could see."

"What did you see when you looked outside?"

She felt like saying, sky, trees, grass...everything but what this interview was about. She held herself back. "I didn't see anyone running from the scene. No movement. And Ian surely wasn't moving. He'd fallen over."

"You screamed."

"Tried my best."

"You brought Tony and Gina running. Where did Tony come from?"

"From behind me."

"From inside the house?"

"Think so."

"How long after you screamed did he arrive?"

"Under a minute."

"Where did Gina come from?"

"Behind me and to my left? Around the corner of the house, I think."

"How long did it take her to get to you?"

"Hard to say...maybe two minutes?"

"Close. Tony and Gina could have been together somewhere."

"Doubt it."

"Why?"

"Just don't think so."

"You touch anything?"

"No."

"Maybe try and revive the victim?"

"Wish I had."

"No, you don't."

"Yes, I do."

"There was nothing you could have done."

"Thanks for trying to make me feel better."

"Did you see the gun?"

"No. But I knew he was shot."

"How?"

"That noise I heard." She shuddered. "And, of course, there was that hole in his back."

Rob heard a commotion coming from the direction of the kitchen—wailing. His abs crunched involuntarily. Linda. He felt so very sorry for Ian's mother.

Nellie usually came home from school through the back. Afternoon snacks were always in the kitchen. But today there were cop cars in front of the house again, and the way to the back was blocked. It was gross having police cars at your house all the time. Kids at school were starting to say mean things.

She opened the front door, and that's when she heard the most horrible noise. Like an animal being killed by another animal on one of those educational channels. She crept through the foyer, past the stairs. She needed to find out what was going on, but no need to hurry, right?

Right in front of her, Detective Dumont and Aunt Becki came out of the library. Both with gritted teeth, frown lines. It wasn't a good sign when adults looked like that. Usually adults tried to not look upset.

"Oh...Nellie...honey," Aunt Becki said. "Let's go upstairs and play in your room."

"What's going on?"

"It's Aunt Linda. Her son is...gone. She's so sad right now. And there's nothing you or I can do. Gina and Tony are there to comfort her. Probably Aunt Mandy too. And Detective Dumont will help out as much as he can."

"Where's Mom?"

"Don't know, but I'm sure she'd want you to come upstairs with me." Aunt Becki reached out and led her by the shoulders to the stairs.

"No. I want to know what's going on." She twisted away from Aunt Becki and started down the hall again.

Detective Dumont was in the kitchen. He blocked her view. She was just ducking under him when—

"Nellie!" It was Mom's voice.

Nellie whirled around.

Mom was standing in the foyer, a bag of groceries in each hand. "Listen to your Aunt Becki. She only wants what's best for you, I'm sure."

Nellie never disobeyed Father. That would just be stupid. And she always listened to Mom for a different reason.

Chapter 28

Tony walked into the study and set his gun down on the desk. "I expect you'll want this."

Rob looked up into hard eyes. He reached for the revolver and sniffed it. No doubt about it—it hadn't been fired recently. He opened the cylinder and spun it, counting the bullets. All there.

"I thought you Bond types carried semis."

"Semis jam a lot. You get six sure shots with a revolver." Tony sat in the chair opposite and leaned forward. "I don't need a semi. I never miss."

Rob thought he had never heard a colder voice. He watched as a hard smile worked its way across Tony's face.

"If you blues practiced more you wouldn't need semis, either. Irresponsible to spray bullets around."

The smug bastard. Rob felt his face go red.

"Come off it, Rob. I know you're pissed about Gina and me. Well, I'm pissed about Gina and you too."

"What the hell—"

"Did you honestly think she would have any time for you after what you did to her years ago? Get real. And stop taking it out on me."

Rob felt the fury build. "Get out," he said.

"Gladly." Tony rose from the chair.

"And don't leave the house."

"Wouldn't think of it." Tony paused in the doorway. "Someone has to figure out what's going on around here."

Rob swore. He scowled down at the revolver, and it took everything in him not to throw it across the room.

Mandy walked slowly into Gina's room and sat down on the bed. She rested her cane against the side.

"How are you faring, Gina?"

She could see the dark circles under Gina's eyes framed by an abnormally pale face. The red shirt, which usually suited her, made her look washed out today. Gina would always be pretty, but right now she looked haunted.

"All right, I guess. Considering. This is a nightmare. I feel like I'm walking through a play."

Mandy nodded. She sighed deeply. Her eyes followed Gina to the window where she was standing. Why did Mandy get the impression of Rapunzel looking out the tower window?

"How's Linda?" Gina's voice shook.

"Quieter now," Mandy said. "Jerry is with her. I gave her one of my Ativans."

"That should help."

Mandy nodded. "It always helps me."

Gina continued to stand looking wistfully out the window.

"Come sit here, Gina. I have something to tell you."

Gina looked over. She turned and walked to the bed, then sat down to face her aunt.

"I didn't tell anyone Tony was adopted because it wasn't done legally." She saw the flush cross Gina's face.

"Hear me out now. Don't judge me yet." Mandy took a deep breath. This was important. She had to say this right. Tony's happiness depended on it.

"You know I used to teach in Vancouver."

Gina nodded.

"It was a high school on the North Shore. One of my students got pregnant at seventeen. She came to me for help. She was a bright young thing, very pretty. She hid her pregnancy well over the winter term and gave birth at the end of August. She told everyone—including her parents—that she was working at a resort for the summer. We took a cabin in the Kelowna area where my old college roommate worked as a doctor. I took the baby home, and that's how I got Tony."

Gina's eyes were saucers. "No one knew?"

Mandy shook her head. "I promised. That was the one condition. My student wouldn't even allow a legal adoption, she was so afraid to have any paper traced to her."

"How sad," Gina said.

"Not for me." Mandy smiled. "I got my baby boy. And you've got to remember—things were different back then. It wasn't cool to be a single mother. This girl was destined for a university, and a baby would have changed everything. For me, it was a dream come true."

"What a risk to take."

"Not so great. My name is on the birth certificate. That's the way the birth-mother wanted it. And that's why Tony never knew."

Mandy thought back to that time in the mountains. A cabin, they called it, although it really was like a summer home with all the conveniences. It had been a hot summer, she remembered, with little rain. The flies had been a problem. And the endless time on their hands. She cleared her throat.

"When Tony turned eighteen, of course the adoption didn't matter anymore. I didn't have to worry about losing him, about some agency coming to take him away. I probably should have told him then, but...there didn't seem a good reason to."

Gina sat still for a moment. "The announcement, during the reading of the will. How did Grandmother find out?"

Mandy sighed. "She knew your uncle was infertile. He'd had a bad case of mumps as a teenager. So it was either adoption, or I had an affair." Mandy smiled. "Even she didn't suspect me of that. I was crazy about your uncle, everyone knew that."

There was a sad moment as she reflected on the past.

"I've never regretted it, not for a second. He was always my son from day one. Always will be. You will understand that when you are a mother. There is nothing I wouldn't do for him—nothing. You think a mother bear is fierce." She felt her voice grow hard.

Gina reached across to take her hand.

"But Gina," Mandy's eyes were compelling. "Remember that. That's what makes this place so dangerous. I'm not the only mother here."

Rob put the phone down. The pistol was unregistered, like so many of the guns up here. There was something about the people who lived in the near north, a streak of bloody independence. Then a thought hit him. Damn and blast! How could he have forgotten? He reached for the cell and started punching numbers.

Jeremy Davis was born and bred in the city and despised it. Since day one, he had asthma. The smog and traffic were like a toxic prison to him. As a kid he had spent his summers on a puffer, throwing stones down sewer grates, envying the kids that got to go up north to the family cottages. When he graduated from the police college five years ago, it was a no-brainer. Huntsville—they needed cops, and he didn't need a puffer.

At first he bunked in the basement apartment of a fellow officer. Two years later, he was able to buy his own little bungalow in a small subdivision in the country. Forest surrounded him on three sides. Since then he had acquired a wife and a dog. Except for the brutal blizzards in winter, life was good.

Jeremy swung the cruiser off Muskoka 13 and onto a small laneway. The Best property was in a ritzy part of cottage country, and although Jeremy wasn't in that league, he'd been through the lakes a number of times on his friend's bass fishing boat. Summer homes of the rich and famous lined the rocky shoreline boasting of wealth. Calling these places cottages was like calling the Taj Mahal a summer camp.

Jeremy reached the end of the drive and eased the cruiser to a stop. Ahead stood a ranch bungalow, probably from the seventies. It was low and long, and looked a little run-down. There was no other vehicle in the driveway.

Jeremy got out of the car and put on disposable gloves. He looked down at the earth for recent tracks. Someone had used the drive during that rain storm last week, he concluded. The ground had been carved and then had dried in ridges. He could make out tire marks, like that of an off-roader...SUV of some sort.

He walked to the front door. *They* would call it the back, of course. On properties such as this, everyone called the lakeside the front even if the obvious entrance faced the road. Some stupid rich person's fancy.

He tried the brass knob on the door. It spun and opened—not even locked. Jeremy shook his head. *Silly rich people.* He moved into the hallway, seeking the kitchen. That was the best place to start looking for occupancy.

At the end of the panel-lined hall stood a seventies Hollywood kitchen right out of one of those sitcoms. He flicked on the big centre light. Jeremy went first to the coffeemaker. Filter still in it with used grounds. Cold, but they weren't mouldy. That told him something.

Then he went to the avocado fridge. *Why in hell would anyone make a colour like that? Let alone buy it.* He surveyed the contents. Homo milk, opened. He picked up the container, opened it and sniffed. Still fresh.

Jeremy felt the cellphone in his pocket vibrate. One hand reached for it. "Yeah, someone's been here recently," he said into it. "Got some good tracks from an SUV, and the milk's fresh. Hold on a sec—"

The overhead light was behind him, so his shadow ran the length of the cupboards. Silently, another shadow approached his. His hand went to his nightstick as he spun around.

Chapter 29

Jeremy summed up the male intruder. Tall, slim, youthful, blond, dressed in a white shirt with a V-neck sweater, in that cheesy diamond pattern that was everywhere these days. He put away his nightstick. "Who're you?"

"Seeing as I never let you in—yet here you are spilling milk all over the floor—same to you."

"Police." He pulled out his ID and shoved it in the man's mug. "One more time, who are you?"

"Andrew McCarthy."

"Not your place of residence."

"Nope."

"Why are you here?"

"Picking up a few things."

"Family?"

"Hilary was a friend."

"You say 'Hilary *was* a friend.' As in you know she's dead?"

"As in I *do* know she's dead, and also as in the friendship's been over for some time."

"Got a rag or something?" Jeremy barked.

Andrew reached under the sink, pulled out a dishcloth and tossed it over.

Jeremy swiped the floor quickly. Then Andrew led him through an archway to an oblong room. He got a dusky view of the lake churning up whitecaps on the other side of the double wall of windows.

The men sat down, and Jeremy indicated the overturned hardcover on the kidney-shaped coffee table between them. "So you were reading?"

"Long trip from Toronto. Thought I'd bunk here overnight and head out in the morning."

"There's no car in the driveway. How did you get here?"

"Took the train from Toronto and a taxi from Huntsville."

"You don't drive?"

Andrew tilted his head. "No need. I live in a civilized part of the world."

"How did you find out about Ms. Best?"

"Funny, really. My boyfriend told me. He was at his grandmother's house, attending her funeral, and a few days later, Hilary's body was found outside."

Jeremy pulled out his notebook and clarified. "Your boyfriend?"

There was no way any food prep was going to happen. No way anyone would head out to a restaurant for supper, either. Becki decided she'd order pizzas and set up a small buffet in the dining room. Nellie, at least, shouldn't go hungry.

She sat in the living room and waited for the knock on the front door, her arms wrapped in a self-hug. Too many deaths. And at least two of them violent. She knew Godmom, Hilary Best and Ian, would go on—call it whatever you like. But the pain of loss remained with the living.

Most people are not able to communicate with their loved ones after death. Well, some people do gab away...it's just...typically...there's no response. Becki felt blessed. "Mom, right now would be a good time to drop in. No one's here."

What wouldn't I do for my one and only daughter?

"Come back to life?"

Rephrasing. What wouldn't I do that's within my means?

"Can you stop this nightmare? Can you stop this killer?"

You think there's just one killer?

"Yes."

Hmmm. Wish I could do something, but I can't do a thing. You can, darling.

"What can *I* do?" After a few minutes, Becki assumed Mom was giving her the look. "You think I'm not trying? I've searched and searched. And searched again. Poured over everything in my head. What I need is a new angle."

Well...here's a suggestion. You know when you enter a quality hotel room and everything looks absolutely perfect?

"You mean those fluffy bathrobes hanging in the closet, herbal tea bags sitting on the tray next to the coffeemaker, toilet paper folded into points..."

Along those lines. Luxurious broadloom, rich mahogany furniture, gleaming marble—

"Right."

After you've been living there in the room a few days, what changes?

"Nothing."

So it might seem. If you wear one of those bathrobes, it's replaced. Tea bags get replenished. But something does change. Think about it— after a few days, the room doesn't look quite so perfect anymore, does it? You notice that wee bit of mould growing in the shower.

"You're saying I should look for a wee bit of mould?"

I'm saying, in time, any wee bit of mould that was previously invisible will jump right out at you.

Carla closed the book. They were close to the end, but Nellie fell asleep. Carla slid out of Nellie's bed, tucked the covers up and contemplated her angel in the lamplight. Tawny skin, tendrils of hair winding over the pillow, her button nose, her fragile eyelids, the sweet mouth of an angel of a child.

She gently pulled the door to the room closed. Nellie—first in her heart, first in all her choices. But they said in the event of an airplane emergency, the *mother* should put on the oxygen mask first, then see to her *child*, and put on his or her mask. That was because if the mother passes out from lack of oxygen, she can't save her child.

Carla entered her own room which looked bigger sans Reggie. She knew she should start to get ready for bed—brush her teeth, floss, wash her face. *Boring.* And in the end, pointless. Right? What had proper nightly routine done for her so far? For that matter, how about her efforts at being a dutiful daughter, and her years and years of wifely devotion? Things having progressed as they did over the last week or so, Carla realized how right it was for her to stand up strong—for herself.

She took the two decorative pillows off the queen-size bed and piled them on the chest at the foot of the bed, then turned down the covers. While pulling off her sweater, then her jeans, she came to a resolution—knew exactly what she had to do—reclaim all that was hers. All her power. To do so, she had to make sure that no-good husband of hers stayed away from Nellie.

She walked into the en-suite. Found further direction while standing over the counter and facing the vanity mirror. First she'd revise her statement about Hilary Best's murder—add to the record Reggie had disappeared that night for over an hour. Then she'd figure out where the bastard was hiding. The police seemed more than just a little dense and definitely needed her help finding him. But, once found, things would turn around for her and Nellie. *Yes!* The slight woman with the nasty facial bruises punched the air.

Chapter 30

Rob looked across at the tearful young man and shifted uncomfortably. *Who does the guy remind me of? Oh yes, that slick blond guy in Brideshead Revisited...what was his name?*

"Why would I kill Ian? I loved him." Andrew's voice cracked. "You people don't understand..." He looked away dramatically. "Yes, I had a few flings—we all do in show biz—but they don't mean anything. I *lived* with Ian, for crissake. We had a *life* together."

He blew his nose loudly into a tissue.

The air in the room was stifling. Rob felt himself go stiff and business-like. "Tell me about your relationship with Hilary Best."

Jeremy put his elbows on the desk and leaned forward.

"I met her at a cougar bar in midtown about six months back. Yes, I'm gay, but I'm actually bi, which Ian hates. Oh God, Ian—" His voice broke again. "You may not believe this, but I have been truly faithful to Ian with respect to other men. I don't do the bath-house thing at all—it's creepy. But I do miss women and occasionally—"

Rob interrupted. "About Hilary."

A pause.

"Right. I liked Hilary. We had a similar interest in art photography which isn't very common, if you know what I mean. She wasn't predatory the way some of them can be. She seemed...vulnerable in a way. Very sensitive. We met at her condo, and I came up here a few times. She didn't have any children, and she liked to baby me. People probably thought we were mother and son or that I was her kid brother." Andrew grinned with satisfaction.

Rob was starting to hate him now too.

"After a while, she started putting off dates. I didn't mind because Ian was acting up and, well, it wasn't good on the set. I kind of got the impression someone else was in the picture, someone more her age and nasty. Guess I was right. The dirty bastard. Did he kill Ian too? But why? Why kill Ian?"

So he didn't know about Reggie and Hilary, Rob mused. *Interesting, how lives intertwine.*

"So what were you doing at the cottage?"

Andrew looked off. "Just picking up a few things. Sweaters and things. I couldn't find the watch she gave me and thought I might have left it there."

Rob looked at him hard. *The watch she gave him, well, isn't that in character? Probably knew about the jewellery. Probably searching the place for anything valuable she may have left behind, the little shit.*

"What type of watch?"

Andrew hesitated. "A Raymond Weil."

Whatever the hell that was. "How do you spell that?"

"W-E-I-L, I think."

Rob wrote it down. "Describe it."

"Gold oblong face. Black band. Last year's, I think."

"Digital or analogue?"

Andrew looked shocked. "Don't be ridiculous. Digital went out with the Disco age. My watch has Roman numerals. And a sapphire stem."

Rob gritted his teeth. "Did you find it there?"

"No." Andrew reached into his pocket. "I found this one instead."

Rob stared down at the watch in his hand…Reggie's watch found at the Muskoka cottage. What the hell did it mean? How long had it been there? Time to talk to Carla again. Rob signalled for the constable at the door.

"I can't believe you never met Andrew."

Gina sat on the front porch watching Tony pace the length of it. It seemed to be the only place free of cops.

"Ian never opened up to me, you know that. He wouldn't be so keen to display the other half of his life." Tony was frowning. He stopped pacing for a moment and stared out across the lawn.

"You saw their TV show, though. You know what he looks like."

"Yeah, once or twice." He mumbled, disinterested. "I've got to get away from here."

Gina shifted uneasily. "Rob said we weren't to leave the house."

"They always say that." He swung around violently. "Look, Gina, think. Where would Reggie go? Where would he hide? He's got to be out there somewhere. I don't believe he left the country."

"Do you think he did this?" Gina looked aghast.

"To Ian? No. Oddly, I don't." He frowned again. "The first one—that was in character. That might have been him. But this...no, I just don't get it." He slapped a hand against the porch pillar. "Can't stand being cooped up like this."

Gina stared at him and felt her heart jerk. What on earth had she been thinking? This wasn't a man who was going to get married and settle down. Tony couldn't stand being stuck for a few days in an old rambling house with the woman he loved...how the heck was he going to react to being chained to one woman forever? Even if they did get married, what would life possibly be like with Tony running off every week to some new adventure?

She continued to stare at him, at his long, lean body and strong profile. Her heart lurched again. *Is love enough?* She used to think so. She used to think everything else would just fall in place if you loved someone enough.

Tony loved her, she knew. But he wouldn't be able to live her carefree downtown lifestyle of dinners out and being seen at all the trendy openings. She couldn't imagine him putting up with that at all.

But how could she live his lifestyle? Who even knew what that was? She slumped down on the porch bench in misery.

"I can't do a damned thing here with blues crawling all over the place. Look Gina, you've got to cover for me."

Gina looked up dully to find Tony glaring at her. "What?"

"I've got to leave for a while. Can you make it seem as if I'm still here? Maybe—" His eyes looked off in the distance then clicked in. "Yeah. Can you go up to my bedroom in the attic? Make it seem as if we are both in there...people will believe that. You can read or something. Give me two, three hours if you can."

Gina felt her jaw drop.

"I need this, Gina." He pleaded in a low voice. "I need to talk to certain people who can help. But I need to do it away from here where no one can listen in. Be a sport, will you? Cover for me."

Gina gazed at Tony solemnly then nodded. So now she was a good sport. What compensation. She rose slowly from the bench and moved to the door without looking at him.

"Don't be too long," she said softly.

But he was already gone.

Chapter 31

Becki realized she was delirious as she sped toward her destination. *Car forty-nine, driven by Rebekkah Green, careens into the hospital parking lot.* Ya, she'd use the word *careen*. She swung open the door. *Got keys? Wallet with health card?*

She staggered toward the emergency entrance. Stopped once. Bent over. Wretched. *Wonderful. Okay. Black and white chequered flag ahead. Finish line—one hundred thousand paces to the sliding emergency doors.*

Once inside, things blurred. She thought she spotted a track official, or maybe a triage nurse, who fortunately also seemed to spot her, and in the wink of an eye she was led through another gateway, and the kindness of the man's voice made her feel safe. Soon she felt something soft meet her skin, and it felt so comfortable to be lying down and to be congratulated over and over again on her win.

"So here we all are once again," Carla pronounced. "A pathetic group. All we do is sit around the table and pretend to eat." She wanted them all to leave. To go home. To leave her alone with Nellie. To start over. But she couldn't just say that.

"No need to make things even worse than they are." This from Gina, who always seemed determined not to let conversation turn maudlin. But her voice held a gentle tone nonetheless. "It's a good sign, don't you think, that we're hanging in *together*?"

"Here, here," brother-in-law Gord said.
"But when will it be over?" Mandy asked.
"Doesn't matter anymore," Linda moaned.
Jerry put his arm around his wife.

Carla sympathised with Linda, but not to the point of, *Yes, this is the absolute end of the world. Let's everyone lie down and play dead. No way!*

She waited to see if big brother Jerry would also hold strong. He didn't disappoint. He shot invisible daggers at Andrew, who'd been invited to join the family for lunch—out of propriety more than anything genuine. Andrew was sort of part of the family. It was just a case of sometimes more than others. And at the moment, he was on the outs as a suspect in the death of Jerry and Linda's only son. Lucky for him, the most likely suspect at large was still her very own husband. *Fucking Reggie!*

"Where's Tony, hon?" Anna asked Gina, breaking into Carla's thoughts. "Didn't see him at breakfast this morning."

"Not feeling well. Flu or something," Gina said.

Good girls don't make good liars. There's a fact for Wikipedia online. "Don't ask me how he could have caught a bug," Carla couldn't help but comment, "cloistered here."

"And Becki?" Anna asked.

"Don't know."

"Haven't seen her."

"Ya, where is she?"

"Probably taking a break," Carla said. "She must be so sick of us by now."

"Mom, may I please be excused?" Nellie asked.

She said please, so even if it didn't look like her daughter'd quite managed to swallow her last mouthful of grilled cheese, Carla said, "Sure, sweetie."

Dr. Crosby, who happened to be gorgeous with greying hair, tanned skin and startling blue eyes, said, "Food poisoning."

"That does it," Becki said. She sat up straighter in her hospital bed. "Eating's out."

"Well, you might want to avoid certain foods. What did you eat that nobody else at the house ate? Say, at breakfast?"

"Something nobody else ate. Let me think. Well...don't want to admit it, but no one else said *yes* to vegetarian sausages...with their eggs."

"Maybe your vegetarian sausages were past the recommended eat-by date. Not a large clientele for something like that in Langdon Hills. Name of the store?"

"Don't remember," she said. Humiliated—a middle-aged woman in a shapeless gown that tied in the back, if you could reach the back—in front of this virile, blue-eyed doctor. "S-s-sorry." She felt close to irrational tears.

His voice soothed. "Don't worry, I understand. Things have been bad for friends of the Ferreros like you. A lot has happened, hasn't it? Starting with Fiorenza. You know, that was hard on me too because I was her doctor."

Becki found his commiseration comforting. "Hate cancer," she declared.

"Me too," he said. "Hate cancer." Pause. "But why bring that up? Do you have cancer? Is there something more I can do for you while you're here?"

Wow...weird. "No. I mean Godmom."

"Fiorenza?"

One heck of a lousy memory! How many patients could he have to keep track of in a town the size of a...postage stamp?

"You've got incorrect information," he said, interrupting her thoughts.

"What?"

"Can't say more." He threw up his hands. "Check your source."

"My source..." She stared into space.

"Okay?" he asked, withdrawing. "Can I leave you alone now?" He stood. "A nurse will be in soon and..." He backed out of the room.

Becki remembered exactly who told her Godmom had cancer. And she'd passed the information along herself to Gina and Tony. Like it was Gospel.

Chapter 32

Gina paused at the doorway. She had been wrestling with this dilemma for hours…wondering what was best. Would Linda want company? Would she want to talk about what had happened? Finally, Gina decided that if something happened to someone she loved, it would be a whole lot worse if others just ignored it.

She knocked softly on the side of the doorframe.

A small voice said, "Come in."

Linda was lying on the bed on her back. There was no one else in the room.

"Aunt Linda…I'm just so sorry." Gina felt her voice break.

Linda looked up from the bed. Her eyes were swollen, and her mascara was smudged. Somehow, her hair was still perfect. How did she do that?

"I just can't take it in, Gina. Ian—my beautiful, harmless Ian. Gone." Her voice was low and hoarse.

Gina walked in tentatively. She stopped at the end of the bed then turned and sat on the corner of it.

"I know. I can't believe it, either. Where's Jerry?"

Linda shrugged. She seemed disinterested.

Gina continued. "Ian was…well, he was always good to me. He was a great older cousin and a good man."

"And talented," Linda added.

"Very talented," Gina said. "I love his show." *Loved*, she should have said. It wouldn't be the same without him. They sat in silence for a moment. "He actually introduced me to the producers at the station, did you know? He helped me get my start."

Linda smiled weakly. "Isn't that just like him?"

Gina grabbed on to the topic. "I was still in university, and Ian suggested I contact this producer guy he knew. Get a head start in the business, he said, before the other graduates started to send out resumes. He was smart about things like that."

Linda nodded. Her eyes started to tear.

"My boy was always bright. He did swell in university...something cum laude, whatever it is. He was meant for the stage or television." She seemed to take strength from this memory. "That Andrew—he was just eye-candy for the camera. It was my Ian who was the brains behind the show."

Gina cleared her throat. "How much do you know about Andrew?"

Linda sniffed. "Enough. He's sweet, I'll grant you that, and very polite. Good dresser. I knew about him and Ian, if that's what you mean. Goodness knows, I'm his mother, and we were very close. He confided in me. Not in Jerry, of course." She sounded satisfied, as if this were a stellar accomplishment for a mother to achieve.

"I mean," Gina searched for words, "what do you know about Andrew's past, Aunt Linda? Do you know his people? Where he's from?"

Linda frowned. "Somewhere in New York, I think. His folks have a cottage up by Gananoque in the Thousand Islands...that's where Ian met him. At some restaurant or other, where Andrew was working."

More likely some gay bar in A-Bay, Gina mused, *but no need to bring that up.*

"Ian was crazy about Andrew from the start," Linda continued. She sat up and motioned for a tissue. Gina lifted the box from the bedside table and handed it to her.

"I can't say I was pleased." Linda blew her nose into the tissue. "Oh, I didn't care about his sexual preference. I've known about that for years. It's just that Andrew always struck me as flighty. I didn't think he'd stick." She folded up the tissue and tossed it to Jerry's side of the bed.

Gina reflected. That was a good description—probably as accurate as she could imagine.

"And with his looks..." Linda continued. "All that temptation. I was worried for Ian."

It had to be said. Gina geared herself. "You don't think he had anything to do with this?"

Linda looked horrified. "Oh no! I didn't mean that. Andrew would never...I'm sure he loved Ian. I just meant that, well, Ian can be a bit possessive. And Andrew is the sort that likes to be taken care of. That can be very attractive to older men and women who want to be needed, you know. I wouldn't be surprised if..." She closed her mouth.

They sat in silence for a moment.

Finally Linda said, "Andrew will be hurting a lot right now. I should go look for him."

Gina nearly choked. From what she had seen of Andrew this afternoon, he was more concerned with finding out the details of Ian's will. But give credit where it is due.

"That's awfully kind of you, Linda. Not everyone would think of that."

Linda nodded with satisfaction. She wiped away a tear. "I'm not a bitch all the time, Gina. Sometimes—when Jerry isn't around—I can be almost human."

Gina laughed and reached over to hug her.

Linda pulled back and looked off in the distance. "Don't ever love too much, Gina. It's hell on earth."

"Linda, I've got to say it. Do you have any idea who might have done this horrible thing? Any idea at all?"

Linda rose and moved slowly to the door. "Not a clue. Wish I did. And you know why."

Gina knew, all right. But she wasn't going to say it out loud.

Rob tried to keep his temper, but it was hard.

"Yes, sir...I know—yes, the press are here...I won't, but you're going to have to...No, not a word until you say...We're working as fast as we can. If you could spare McTaggart..."

He clicked the phone shut and swore.

It rang again.

"Bloody hell, Chris, where are you?" Rob listened to his sergeant. This day had gone from bad to worse. Still no sign of that loser, Reggie. Where the hell was the son-of-a-bitch? Only one person might know, and she wasn't cooperating. Wait a minute...that gave him an idea.

"Get back up here, ASAP. Listen to what I'm thinking." He explained to Chris what he had in mind.

Gina sat on the front porch, gratefully alone. Linda and Andrew were having a cry-fest in the kitchen—oh dear, she shouldn't put it that way. That was cruel. They were genuinely grieving. It's just there was no place for Gina. Her grief was secondary...a quiet thing. So she had discreetly made her way down the hall and out to the world beyond the doors of this fractured family home.

She sat on the bench, half wishing she'd gone for that long walk with her parents. Now, she waited for them to return. No, that was a lie. She was waiting for someone else.

Footsteps brought her out of a dark reverie.

"Waiting for Tony?"

Gina turned in shock. Rob stood in the doorway.

"Don't bother making excuses. I know he's skipped, the bastard. Never could take orders from anyone."

Rob came forward and motioned with his hand. She shifted to make room for him on the bench.

"Will he be back soon?" Rob's voice was gritty. His big body shifted, moving the entire bench.

Gina nodded. She looked straight ahead.

"Do you know where he's gone?"

A pause. She shook her head.

"You telling the truth?"

She turned to look at him. "Of course I am. He didn't tell me because he knew you would ask."

Rob laughed abruptly. "Son-of-a-bitch. Okay, Gina. But do you have any idea what he's doing?"

Gina paused a moment. She looked back at Rob and made her decision. "I think he's getting in touch with some people he knows who might be able to help locate Reggie. Work people."

Rob frowned. He leaned his forearms on his knees. "Yeah, they might be able to, all right." He sounded pissed. "Spooks don't have to go through the same channels we lawmen do."

He made it sound like they were in an old Western. Gina's mouth broke to a thin smile.

They sat in companionable silence for a few moments. Rob appeared to be deep in thought. Finally, he said, "That was clever, your deduction about tracing the victim through the store where she bought the handbag. It's the sort of thing we cops think about."

Gina smiled. "I had a bit of luck. It doesn't always work. As a matter of fact—now that's funny." She paused.

Rob raised one eyebrow.

"About the bag being unique." Gina continued. "Remember I said that thing about how the sales clerks keep track of who buys what, so we don't show up at the same event in the same dress?"

Rob nodded.

Gina looked off in the distance. "It can happen. In fact, it did happen, at the Belle Canto Opera Gala a few years ago. And you'll never guess to whom."

Gina turned to face him now. Yes, she had his interest. Funny that she remembered it now, years later, after never once thinking about it before.

"Hilary walked into the place wearing a super-expensive Givenchy red chiffon gown. Darned if her sister Andrea didn't show up wearing the very same dress. They met each other in the centre of the crowded lobby." She giggled at the memory. "Oh my goodness, you never saw such a scene."

"Hilary didn't like it much?"

"Hilary didn't give a rat's ass—oops. No really, she thought it was a scream. It was Andrea who had a conniption. Apparently, she bought the dress in Palm Springs, so that's how the Toronto store didn't know about it. But there were the two of them, both in blond updos, both looking so alike..." She giggled again.

"What's an updo?" Rob asked.

Gina grabbed her hair with one hand and swept it up onto her head. When she let go, it fell naturally into a mass of chestnut curls halfway down her back.

"So there they were, Hilary laughing and pointing, and Andrea screaming at her like a gutter wench. She took a couple swipes at her with her evening bag—Andrea, that is—swiping at Hilary, who ducked—and finally, Andrea marched out of the place, never to be seen again that night. Hilary stayed and acted like the belle of the ball."

Rob frowned. "So they didn't like each other."

Gina nodded. "People said they were competitive, which is a nice way of putting it, from what I saw."

"I know about competition," Rob muttered.

Gina had the sense to keep quiet. She could see where this line of thought was headed and didn't like it.

"You know about his real work now." It was a rhetorical comment. No need to ask whom Rob was talking about. Gina said nothing. Overhead, a seaplane droned by.

"You okay with it?" Rob was pushing it. The disbelief in his voice was clear.

"No, of course I'm not okay with it," Gina replied. "How could I be okay with it? But it's not my job or my life—it's his. What can I do about it?" Her voice was bitter, and almost immediately she regretted using it.

"Do about what?" A cool voice said at her side.

Rob was on his feet. "You're back," he growled.

Tony nodded, standing with his arms crossed. "And I have news."

Chapter 33

She established when she woke from another of her profound slumbers that day was dwindling by the lack of light on the other side of the industrial hospital window spanning the end wall of her room. The nurse said they were keeping her overnight for observation when all Becki figured she needed was sleep. She guessed there was less demand for hospital beds in Langdon Hills than in Toronto. In Toronto, she'd be booted out on the street already. But here she'd have nurses around each time she woke to threaten to reintroduce her to real food.

She didn't see the need to ever eat again. But she wasn't the sort of person to be a problem patient, so, appetite or no appetite, she was willing to follow Dr. Crosby's orders. Two to four hours without any food or drink at all. *Done.*

Then small amounts of weak, room temperature tea or ginger ale that had been opened for an hour to release the bubbles. Then if she could tolerate that without further upset, the addition of an apple or banana—puree was recommended—after which she could safely move on to other fruits and vegetables, excluding potatoes. As a last step, after six to twenty-four hours at each successive stage, she could choose meat. *Not!*

Or grains. Or even dairy, if she felt daring.

She sipped some flat ginger ale from the plastic cup lingering on the metal table beside her hospital bed and remembered she wanted to phone Gina. Because she had something important to discuss with her. She picked up the receiver then reconsidered the order of her calls. After all, shouldn't she phone her husband first? If the situation was reversed and *he* landed in a hospital bed far from home, wouldn't she want to be the first person he called?

"Hi, honey. How are you?" he asked as soon as he recognised her voice.

"Extreme dieting," she deadpanned. When she thought about the word that described the comic's tone she was trying to take with Karl, it reminded her way too much of *bed panned*.

"Really? Dieting? What for?"

Isn't he charming? That's why I went ahead and married him all those years ago. Well, that and the police chief uniform.

"See," she began, "what happened, Karl, is...I got food poisoning."

"Poison?"

Hearing panic, she quickly clarified, "*Food* poisoning. Had my stomach pumped and everything. And now the good doctor and his trusty nurse cohorts are planning to build my strength up again. Starting all over from the beginning. Like an infant. With mush."

"Oh, honey."

"Not to worry. So how are things on your end?"

He ignored her question. "What was it you ate?"

The line crackled.

"Pardon?" he said.

"Vegetarian sausages."

"All living creatures know they're poison."

"Karl!"

"Sorry. What I mean is, how awful."

He sounded like he really meant it this time.

"Who else got sick?" he asked.

"No one."

"How's that again?"

"What do you think, Karl?" *This is embarrassing.*

"Oh, I see. Couldn't entice anyone else to try your breakfast meat replacements. And so therefore they were spared."

"That's about it."

She must have started to sound more defeated than amused because Karl quickly changed his tactic. "Missing you. Counting the days. You've been gone nine full days now. Way too many to be away from your husband, who loves you."

Maybe she yawned.

"You sure you're okay?"

"Sorry. Running on empty. Literally."

"Hungry," he surmised.
"Noooo!"
Silence.

She regretted shouting at him. "As if I needed another reason to stay stuck in Langdon Hills."

Despite her pessimistic tone, something hopeful was twitching at the back of her brain and making her think that possibly, after doing just one more little thing, the whole frigging ordeal might come to an end. She just needed to pass it by Gina first.

"First thing tomorrow, I'm coming out there to see you," Karl said.

"Don't. I'm fine. Just fine. Hold down the fort for me at home. And I'll be back before you know it."

"Not soon enough."

"If you come here, you'll get dragged into this whole mess. It's bad enough one of us has been ripped from ordinary life and forced to live in the middle of a...a thriller."

"You? And ordinary life?"

"Compared to this."

"You really don't want me to come," he stated.

"No."

"Hmmm."

"Why, *hmmm*?"

"Remember, I said I'd look into Tony and that gun of his you saw? Tony's a fed. Has been for some time. Undercover. Really, the only reason I was able to find out what I did about him is I'm in the biz too. So if he's with you, you're in good hands. But keep this to yourself. That's a must."

"Tony? A fed? Holy smoke! That's good news. I guess. Unless he's—whaddaya call it?—gone rogue."

"Rogue?"

"You know, as in Sarah Palin's book."

"I should come, anyway."

"No! Hey, Karl, it's starting to snow here. First snow of the season. Is it snowing there?"

After a half an hour of convincing him she was fine, she fell asleep again. When she awoke, it was completely dark outside. *Time flies when you're unconscious.*

She dialled Gina's cell over and over. Gina didn't pick up. Each time Becki tried, she was directed to voicemail. Why would Gina turn off her phone? The only thing Becki could do was leave a message.

"Gina, it's Becki. So...I'm the one who's in hospital now. I know. Dumb. Something I ate. Anyway, I discovered something here. By fluke.

My doctor, Dr. Crosby, is...was...Godmom's doctor too. And he happened to let it slip that Godmom didn't have cancer. You believe that? What's it mean, do you think? Was Carla lying? Or was she somehow convinced Godmom had cancer? Weird, huh? So I want to talk to you about it. Call me. Room 27. They're forcing me to stay here overnight. So call anytime. Don't worry how late. Believe me, I'm getting plenty of sleep. And Gina...be careful. Something's seriously not right about this. Okay...bye for now."

    Great fluffy flakes were floating down from the sky on the other side of Nellie's bedroom window. As Mom would say an infinite variety of perfect crystals. Snow meant tobogganing. And snowmen. And skating. And Christmas. But Christmas was still almost three months away.
    She cuddled under the covers with Macho. His face, hands and feet were made of rubber or something, but the rest of him was soft just like her other stuffed animals—the ones who didn't sleep with her—which were lined up at the end of the bed. Sometimes she felt sorry for them way over there, but Mom said she could only have one stuffed animal under the sheets at night, and since Macho was her favourite...Macho's arms were around her, and she made sure the blankets were well under his chin, so he could still breathe. She tucked him in just like Mom tucked her in every night. Finally, when Macho started to snore really loud, she decided it was probably okay for her to fall asleep too.

Chapter 34

Gina stood on the porch between the two titans and waited for Tony to break the tension.

"He's alive," Tony said. "And in Ontario. Used a bank card east of Kingston yesterday. Seems we all forgot one thing."

"What's that?" Rob's voice was grim.

Tony pulled a pack of cigarettes from his pocket. He knocked one out and held the pack over to Rob. For one tense moment, Gina thought Rob was going to smack it away. But he didn't. Gina saw him hesitate, and then he reached over to pull it out.

"Thanks," he mumbled.

Tony snapped open a lighter and lit his own. He snapped it closed then tossed the lighter to Rob, who seemed to be expecting it and caught it easily. It hit Gina suddenly she was watching a scene that had happened many times before in the past between these two.

Tony took a big drag and then let out smoke.

"We forgot Reggie had been married before. His ex lives in Gananoque, and the family have a cottage in the Thousand Islands."

Rob cursed.

"Did you know he had a son? No? Well, he never told me about it either. Kid is about eleven. Mother has sole custody."

Gina watched the two men eye each other.

Finally Rob said, "That it? Just a bank card?"

Tony grunted. "It's more than you came up with."

"Son-of-a-bitch," said Rob.

Gina couldn't tell whether Rob was referring to Tony or the information. The tension was pretty hot on the porch.

"Got an address?" Rob mumbled it around the cigarette in his teeth.

Tony reached in his shirt pocket and pulled out a paper. "Name of ex, town address, cottage address and number of bank machine. Knock yourself out, lawman."

Rob snatched it from his hand then disappeared into the house.

Gina stood looking at Tony.

"You didn't make any friends there."

Tony snorted. "We may both wear white hats, but we're at war. Didn't you know?"

"Mom, have you seen Becki?"

"No, sweetie. I haven't been here. I've just come from the lawyer's with your dad."

Gina watched her mom pour tea from the old china pot. She poured it immaculately, without losing a drop. Gina went to the cupboard for more cups.

"I haven't seen her for hours. I wonder where she went." she said.

"Not far, I'm sure. That nice policeman keeps track of us. Speaking of which," Mom lingered over the cup, "what exactly is going on between you and him? And is that why Tony is so miserable?"

Miserable? Tony was acting miserable? Oh, for crying out loud—and then it hit her like a winter gale. Mom didn't know who Rob was. She didn't remember. Gina's eyes went wide. Mother didn't know Rob was the boy who had caused her to be sent to Vancouver that summer long ago. Oh, crap. What the heck would she say when she found out? Even worse, what would her dad do?

The knock caused Rob to look up from his desk.

"Yes?"

Carla stood in the doorway. She looked better than he'd seen her look the entire week. Her hair was nicely combed, and there was colour in her face. Why hadn't he noticed how good-looking she was before?

"Can I get a day pass for tomorrow? I have a doctor's appointment in Toronto."

Rob stared at her. Carla's face was stony. *Appointment in Toronto, my ass,* he thought. But this was the chance he had been waiting for.

"Just for the day?"

She nodded. "I'll leave early, do my business and get back after dinner at the latest."

Rob leaned back in his chair. He took some time thinking to make it look good. "All right," he said finally. "Take your cellphone, and leave it on."

"Thanks. I'll get Gina to look after Nellie."

"She's in the parlour, I think."

Carla nodded again and moved away with a sway in her hip.

Something wrong with that woman, Rob thought.

"What's wrong, Gina? Are you looking for something?" Carla stood at the door to the front parlour, watching.

"Have you seen my cellphone? I seem to have lost it. It's pink." Gina turned from the couch where she had been lifting pillows.

Carla shook her head. "Try dialling the number."

"Did that," said Gina. She sat down with a thump and a sigh. "It may have run out of juice."

Carla didn't seem concerned. "So use the house phone. The police won't mind."

Gina shook her head. "I was just going to check calls, not make any. If I call work, they'll just make it difficult for me." She sat frowning.

Carla went to the window.

"Will you do me a favour and look after Nellie tomorrow?"

Gina looked over in surprise.

"Well, sure. But where are you going?"

Carla shrugged. "Got a doc appointment in Toronto. Our Sergeant Renfrew of the RCMP is letting me go for the day, can you believe it? I promised to be good and get back around dinner."

Gina was mystified. After that prank of Tony's, she was surprised Rob would let anyone step away from the house, let alone drive to the city.

"Lucky you," she said. "I'd love to get away."

"How long are you going to stay here?"

Gina's head shot up. Why did Carla sound like that? "Only as long as they make me. I have to be back in Toronto next week for work at the latest."

Was that the shadow of a smile? Gina stared. It seemed Carla would be pleased to see her go. But why? Carla had always liked her, she was sure of it. They both loved Nellie, for one thing.

"It's got to be difficult for you with all these people invading your home." Gina chose her words carefully.

They seemed to be the right words.

Carla nodded. "It's not good for Nellie. I can't wait for things to get back to normal."

Normal? With Ian murdered and Reggie missing? Gina stared at the woman in front of her, who stood gazing placidly out the window. It was as if she suddenly didn't know this calm and cool person masquerading as her aunt. What the devil was wrong with Carla?

Chapter 35

Carla had so many reasons to not want them finding Reggie now. Of course, she had to press charges for the last time he beat her, but she didn't feel like going through some court ordeal, didn't want Nellie having to deal with kids taunting her for having a jailbird for a father, didn't want him...*Just best if the bastard stayed missing.*

But before Carla reached the road that led out of town, she picked out a tail on her heel. Which prompted a very unflattering thought. *Rob thinks I'm brain dead.*

She gripped the wheel. *Langdon Hills is a small town. Traffic would have to be labelled slow to non-existent. He knows that. As if I'm not going to notice a vehicle following me from my own street practically to the highway. Firstly, the odds of any two cars twinned in time and place in Langdon Hills is beyond all probability. And secondly, if a miracle of the sort did happen one day, I'd know exactly who it was, and then afterward I'd make a comment about it to that neighbour—I see you were heading out to buy a few cases of Diet Coke on sale at Costco in Orillia at the same time I was yesterday.*

No way was she enough of a bonehead to miss the ambulant police presence and its significance. Not only did it scrap her plan to have a little chat with Reggie and send him off once and for all—before the police caught up with him on Salisbury Island, as threatened in the conversation she overheard between Gina, Tony and Rob—it revealed she was under suspicion. One thing she knew, she'd be in a whole mess of trouble if they caught her skipping town under false pretences.

She shook her head with tight, jerky movements. She decided to teach the cops a lesson. She picked up her cellphone from the passenger seat as if the ringer were signalling an incoming call. She brought it to her ear. The officer behind her, whether it be Rob or one of his cronies, wouldn't dare arrest her for using a mobile device while driving because he was *incognito*.

"Blah blah blah blah blah blah blah," she rattled into the receiver, looking from side to side and at her rear-view while she drove. She made the sounds just so Copman would see her lips moving. She found it amusing so she raised her voice and before long, her *blah blahs* hit ear-splitting pitch. Satisfied, she dropped the phone back onto the seat, turned her car around and headed for home.

Tony leaned against the study door jam.

"Dumont, I've got to go. I've been called in."

Rob snorted. "You're not going anywhere."

Tony laughed. He folded both arms across his chest. "You try telling them that."

Smug bastard, Rob thought. Then he cursed. Damned feds. He could just imagine the calls starting from high up.

"Do you think I want to go now?" Tony said. "With Gina still here and vulnerable?" He ran a shaky hand through thick hair. "Look, Dumont, you gotta look out for her."

Rob was alert now. "You think she's in danger?"

"No," Tony said slowly. "No, not immediately. But I didn't think Ian was, either."

Rob leaned forward. He steadied his voice. "What the hell do you know that I don't?"

"Nothing concrete." Tony hesitated. "I'm not sure. Just a gut feel, maybe, but a strong one. Maybe Becki knows more. Talk to Becki."

"Tony, by God, if you know something—"

"Talk to Becki. I've been trying to, but I can't find her."

Gina sat on the bench at the back of the garden. It had taken some effort to escape from the house without company. But Tony had gone to have a quick word with Rob, so Gina took her chance.

Her parents and Tony's mother were napping. Nellie was getting washed and dressed. Jerry had taken Linda to Ian's hotel to pack up his things. Becki had offered to do it yesterday, but Linda would have none of that. Poor Linda. She needed to hang on to every thread of Ian, every piece of him that was left, for as long as possible. Gina understood.

When all was packed up, he would be physically gone. The feeling of tragedy hung like a thick smog, the steel-town kind which left you with a heavy chest.

Becki was nowhere to be seen today. Funny, that.

But Gina had wanted to be alone to think. She was good at it—thinking. But it took solitude...something that hadn't been available over the last while.

So she let her thoughts go deep, to explore the events that had taken place. She opened her mind to every possibility she could think of.

First, that woman had been murdered. But was that first, really? Or had her grandmother's death been first? Where did the puzzle start? That was the thing. So often in books, murder was the start of the story. Here, a funeral was the start. Or was it?

But you have to start somewhere, she reasoned. *Start with what we know.*

A woman was murdered. She was murdered close to the house and most of the family had opportunity. She was murdered with a baseball bat—Gina shivered—which meant that not everyone could have done the deed. Tony's mother couldn't have. Gina's own parents had an alibi on the high seas. But most everyone else could have done it. But why would they?

Next, look at motive. The woman was well-dressed and attractive. She had a reputation for seeking out younger men. Probably, she was having an affair with Reggie. That would be logical. Although...somewhere Gina remembered something about Linda...something that led her to believe Linda thought Jerry might be involved. Could Jerry have had an affair with her? *That's not kind,* Gina thought, *use her name. Treat her like a person. Could Jerry have had an affair with Hilary?*

Gina looked up into the grey sky. Birds were flying listlessly in circles.

Already it was getting complicated. She'd stick with Reggie for now. Reggie was missing, and that made him involved, for one thing. So—assume Reggie had an affair with Hilary...why was Hilary here? Did he invite her? That seemed unlikely with the whole family here for a funeral and Carla and Nellie close by. Did Hilary follow him up here trying to convince him to meet her? Perhaps Reggie had tried to break off the affair, and Hilary wasn't having any of it. Maybe Hilary was going to tell Carla, and Reggie had to stop her...

Would Reggie care enough to do that? Would he risk a murder rap to keep Carla from finding out about the affair? That didn't make sense. Yes, Carla had the money, actually, Nellie did now, but if this woman

Hilary was so rich she could afford Gucci handbags, why didn't he just go off with her? Gina wondered if anyone else had thought of that. Why would Reggie kill the Golden Goose?

Okay, that was one strike against him being the murderer. Except that Reggie was violent, everyone knew that. Hitting someone over the head in the heat of anger is just something he might do. Right in character. Gina found herself nodding automatically.

So assume the killer is Reggie. Why would Reggie kill Ian? Certainly, Reggie didn't have any love for Ian. He wasn't a blood relative, and Reggie was the sort of insecure man who showed contempt for homosexuals. So he could have done it. He had the psychology. But why?

The most logical reason was that Ian had seen something. In every case, that was the most logical reason for Ian being killed. He saw or knew something about the first murder and was a danger to the killer.

Who else had motive? Gina opened her mind and tried to divorce her personal feelings about the people involved.

Carla. She was an obvious suspect, and her motive would be jealousy. But did Carla care enough about Reggie to risk a murder rap? Gina couldn't see it. Carla was an abused woman herself. Gina was of the belief that Carla hated Reggie and would be glad to be done with him. Let the other woman have him and then Carla would be safe. Besides, Carla would never kill Ian, her own blood nephew. She loved Ian.

So who else? Linda, she supposed, for the first murder. If Hilary was seeing Jerry then Linda just might take a bat to her. Unlike Carla, Linda had every reason to protect her marriage. But—and it was an overwhelming but—Linda would never kill her own son. No, if Linda committed the first murder, someone else must have committed the second and for a completely different reason.

Could there be another reason to kill Ian? Well—actually—yes. Ian was a rich man now. Someone could have killed him for his money, or rather, the money he was due to inherit.

Who would do that? Not his parents, that's certain. But Andrew could have. Andrew was the selfish type who liked a soft life. Andrew might have seen the opportunity to shoot Ian and have the police think it was connected with the first murder. But would Andrew kill in cold blood? She didn't think so. To seek out a pistol and coolly aim it and fire…that took premeditation and nerves of steel. Besides, Andrew could twist Ian around his little finger. He would have the money by just staying with Ian, so why bother with something as risky as murder?

Who would have the steely disposition to complete such a task?

Load, aim, fire...and not miss. Who else had motive? Ironically, someone might say that she and Tony did. They both would inherit more by Ian's death.

So here it comes, she thought. *Deal with it. You've got to think it through.*

What about Tony? What if Tony were having an affair with the woman? What if he tried to call it off? What if she came here to see Tony and was going to threaten him with exposure? Not about their affair. He wouldn't care about that. But about his other job? Would he kill to protect that knowledge from getting out?

He might. Dear God, Gina had to admit he might. But would he kill Ian too? Say Ian had seen something that pointed the finger at Tony. Could Tony kill his own cousin?

Gina felt sick. They weren't blood-related anymore.

What about Tony?

"What *about* Tony?"

Gina gasped and looked up. Tony was standing not five feet away gazing down at her. She hadn't realized she'd said that last line out loud.

"I was just thinking," she said. It was hard to keep the shake out of her voice.

Tony whirled himself down on the bench beside her.

"Look. I've got to go away for a bit."

"Again?" The word was out before she could stop herself.

Tony nodded. "Not my choice. I've been called."

"For how long?"

"A few days. I don't know. Just to Toronto. Not out of the country."

Gina swallowed hard. "Does Rob know?"

A grin. "He does now."

"Well, have a good time." The second the words were out, she realized how idiotic she sounded.

"Look, Gina, stay close to Becki while I'm gone."

Gina looked up at the sky. "I would if I could. Where is she?"

"I don't know. But find her. She knows more, I swear it. And she loves you to pieces, so I know you'll be safe with her."

He stood up with the sinewy grace of a wolf. "I don't know about anyone else."

"Gina, thank God I finally got hold of you," Becki said over the landline and the relief was real. "Where've you been?"

"Where have *you* been?" Gina replied.

"In the hospital. I've been trying to reach you—"

"The hospital?"

"Don't ask."

"Of course, I'm asking. What's wrong?"

"Nothing now, but—"

"I'll be right there. I'll have Nellie with me."

"Hold on!" She tried to listen through the silence on the other end. *Is Gina still there?* "Gina?"

"Yes."

"I think I've given you the wrong impression. I'm fine. Just fine. Long story."

"Coming right over."

"Not necessary. Honestly. I'll be released very soon. And I've got my car sitting right outside in the parking lot. Drove myself in yesterday. It was just a touch of food poisoning. That's all. No reason for you to be concerned."

"Really."

Gina sounds awfully sarcastic for someone as sweet as she.

"Perhaps there's some contaminated food I should throw out before anyone else gets sick."

"No...yes...no..."

"Becki!"

"The vegetarian sausages I offered around at breakfast yesterday. No takers. And I seriously doubt anyone has developed a craving subsequently. But just in case, will you—"

"Certainly."

"Discretely?"

"Of course."

"Gina?"

"Yes?"

"I have something important to say. And the more I think about it, the more worked up I get. In fact, unless you're able to talk me out of it, as soon as I hang up, I'm calling Rob. Tony and Karl too."

"Why?"

"Your grandmother didn't have cancer after all. Not according to Dr. Crosby."

"You're the one who told me it was cancer."

"I know."

"And Carla confirmed it later."

"Right. It was Carla who told me Godmom had cancer. And Dr. Crosby just told me she didn't. So there you have it. Two different stories. Did she have cancer or not? Do we believe Carla or Dr. Crosby? Is cancer the cause of death? Did she die of natural causes? Or—"

"Becki, you're scaring me. You make it sound so sinister. Don't you think the whole yes or no cancer thing is a misunderstanding?"

"Which brings me to exactly what I want from you—your advice. Because I'm not an official member of your family—"

Gina started to object, but Becki cut her off.

"I'm not. So I'm torn about how to proceed. I decided it was best to run it by you. And ask is there reason to be suspicious of Carla? Is she covering up for Reggie, perhaps? Should we tell the police?"

Gina seemed at a loss.

Becki let out a sigh. "I should add I remember wondering why there weren't any prescriptions or drugs of any kind in Godmom's room when I helped your mom clean it out. I even asked Carla about it 'cause she was the one who was living with Godmom. You know what Carla said?"

"What?"

"She said she cleared out the drugs earlier so Nellie wouldn't happen upon them and poison herself.

"Good idea."

"I thought so too at the time."

"You know, Grandmother could have fibbed about cancer to Carla, although for the life of me, I can't think why she'd do it…"

"Endless possibilities."

"Hmmm…"

"So should I talk to Rob? To Tony? To Karl?"

"Let me think."

Becki waited a few seconds.

"No, poor Carla. She doesn't need more heartache on top of what she's been through. I mean, what if it's…nothing? How about if I talk to her and try and get a feeling for what's going on? I'm pretty intuitive, you know. A nose for weather and all that."

"Sure," Becki said. "And I'll be there soon. Let me know what you get out of her, 'kay?"

Chapter 36

"That didn't take long," Rob yelled at Carla when she breezed past the library door.

Carla backed up, poked her head in the room. "What?"

"Thought you were on your way to Toronto."

"Was. Luckily I didn't get too far because my doctor's office called to reschedule. Seems a time slot opened up at his dentist's and he jumped on it. Naturally, my esteemed doctor's scaling units, white amalgam fillings, and root canals are number one priority. No problem for us little people to reshuffle our agendas."

"You sound bitter."

"Just an inconvenience."

"Are you fond of your *esteemed* Toronto doctor?"

"He's all right."

"Must be more than just all right for you to keep going to him even if he's all the way in Toronto."

"You know I lived there for a while. Couldn't be bothered switching doctors. Don't go often. Just my annual check-up. Then I do a bit of shopping."

"That's what your appointment was, then—an annual check-up?"

Carla eyed him suspiciously.

"You're okay?" he specified.

"Just my annual check-up," she repeated. "Mother died of cancer, so…keeping on top of things."

"But Nellie has a doctor in town?"

The fingers of her right hand holding the strap of her purse tapped. "Of course she does."

"And your mother?"

"She does—did too."

"Can I have their names and addresses?"

"For crying out loud, Rob. What's with the third degree? You've known me and my family since I was a kid. You already know everything about me."

"Not the name of your doctor."

"And that's going to help how?" She sidled up to his desk. Not *his* desk, actually. She bent to look at him, steadied her brown eyes on his.

No two ways about it, Carla was looking one whole heck of a lot better. The bruises on her face were nearly imperceptible now. In fact, she was hotter than before bastard Reggie beat her up. Like she was blossoming or something…finally out from under his control.

"Just doing my job," he said. "Being thorough. Leaving no rock unturned."

"Bending yourself in two looking under rocks, Rob? Bet Tony doesn't do that." She smirked.

"Tony?" he snarled in irritation. But seconds later, he felt like smacking his lips with satisfaction. Because he recognized an important slip when he heard one.

Carla knows Tony's a cop, damn it! And she shouldn't, should she? Tony would never tell her. Nor would Gina. So she overheard our conversation last night. Therefore she must also know we're on to Reggie. And that's what's really going on here.

He let out a groan. Carla had been on her way to warn the bastard, but she'd spotted her tail. *Stupid, stupid broad! What do women see in men like that? No matter what they do to them! It's like they can't stop trying to save them.*

He looked up at her with real pity in his eyes. But still he needed to call her doctor to confirm this new theory.

"I'm sorry, Carla, you're going to have to cooperate whether you feel like it or not. I need those names and addresses."

She pulled away. "If you must," she said. "I've got business cards upstairs in my files. I'll bring them down later."

Rob could have sworn she batted her eyes. "Not later. Now."

Not only did he need them immediately, he figured she might respond to masculine forcefulness. Maybe that's what she dug about Reggie Williamson—his authority. *Of course, Gina is a much better catch than Carla, and if I could have Gina again, I'd jump at the chance, but in the meantime...*

In the meantime, he enjoyed watching Carla's butt flounce out of the room.

Upstairs, Carla braced herself on her dresser, leaned in and checked out her reflection in the mirror. She had to admit she was looking fine, but, hell, the day wasn't going so well. *Cut off at every damned turn!*

Okay. She knew how to stall.

Oh...Rob. I forgot! Shoot, you're not going to make me climb up the stairs again, are you? Not with this cast on. I'll bring them down next time. Promise.

Yes, that would be perfect. *Not all men are as hard to deal with as Reggie.*

Suddenly, in the mirror, she saw someone standing outside her room. She hiked in a breath.

But it was just Gina who filled the gap between door and doorframe. She tapped lightly. "Sorry to bother you."

"That's okay." Carla turned. "Nellie's all right?"

"Absolutely. No problem. We were playing in her room, and I saw you walk by. Nellie didn't see you. She was facing the other way. Anyway, I wondered if everything was okay with you."

"Why wouldn't it be?"

"You asked me to babysit Nellie. You were supposed to be gone most of the day. And now you're back already."

"No biggie. Doctor had to reschedule. I'll take over with Nellie. Just give me a minute."

"No, it's not that..." Gina took in a breath. "We're having fun. Take your time." She turned to go then changed her mind. "Becki called this morning."

"Oh? Where the hell is she, anyway?"

"In hospital."

"What's up?"

"Food poisoning."

"Ha! If she can't stomach vegetarian, maybe she should drop down a level to macrobiotic."

"Not funny, Carla. Becki was really ill."

"Right. Sorry."

Carla didn't understand Gina's concern. Becki wasn't even her real aunt. And they were nowhere near close in age. In fact, she was kinda pissed at how close Gina and Becki seemed to be. "Nellie and I will make a point to go see her this afternoon," she said in a conciliatory tone.

"No need. She's coming home any minute now."

What does Gina mean 'home'?

"And I'd like to talk to you about something she said on the phone this morning."

Carla's ears pricked. "Ya?"

"Becki said Grandma's doctor, Dr. Crosby, claimed she didn't have cancer."

"What?" Carla's eyes widened. "How can that be? Is the man deranged?"

"He said, 'Check your source.' Which means *you*. You told us she had cancer."

"Because that's what she had. That's what she told me. And she didn't want anyone else to know. Just us who lived in the house with her."

"Well, now we have two stories, and they don't match. It's really weird, don't you think?"

"I'll say. Maybe Mother had a different doctor for her cancer treatments or something."

"Wouldn't her family doctor be kept advised?"

"I suppose...But you know how stubborn Mother could be. If she wanted something kept secret..."

Gina's eyes brightened with an idea. "Carla, it was you who tended to her, so what was the name of the doctor on her prescriptions?"

"Hell if I know."

"Didn't you read the labels?"

"Not the fine print, for Christ's sake."

"And you said you threw out the bottles."

"Explained that."

"You know, a lot of us had an odd feeling about Grandma's death...right from the start."

"What do you mean, *a lot of us*?"

"Becki, Tony, me."

"Whatever for?" Carla asked with increasing impatience. "Mom was old," she said, feeling her face flush. "She was sick—"

"She was found with a pillow on her head. It was you who found her like that. And you can stand there and tell me you never thought a thing of it?"

"What can I say? Maybe she twitched...and it fell on her head." Now she looked at Gina through slitted eyes. "You don't know how awful it was to find Mom like that. I described everything to the ambulance guys and to Rob when he came by and to everyone else who wanted to know. Even though I hated to relive it all. Then each and every one of them determined Mom died of natural causes. And now she's laid to rest." Her eyes filled with tears. "Why are you dragging it all up again?"

Chapter 37

Tony drove the Audi like a Formula 1 racer to Toronto. *Of all the times to be called away...*

While driving, he brooded. These crimes pointed to two people, but which one was it? If it were the right person—and oh yes, there was a right person to be guilty, at least for the family—then everything would be okay for now. But if Tony were wrong...if the wrong person was guilty...

Transports slipped behind him like little toys in the distance. The sign for the 400 went by in a flash. Tony drove the manual transmission with skill, but even he had to admit this was reckless. Thing was, it was even more reckless leaving Gina back at the house.

He cursed again.

When he got close to Barrie, he pulled off the highway into a service station. He sat for a moment watching people come and go from the coffee shop. What was the worst that could happen? If he didn't respond to the work call, they could sack him. *Fine with him.* Whoa, that made him suck air. Yeah, it was true. They could sack him, and he wouldn't mind a bit. In fact, it would make everything a whole lot simpler. *Bloody hell.*

Funny how only a few years ago his job had been everything. He had thrived on the excitement, the adrenaline rush every time he got a new assignment. The travel was a bonus, and he couldn't count how many times he got a kick out of playing with all the tools of the trade. He had liked carrying a concealed weapon. He had liked working behind the scenes, and damn, he was good at it. How, recently, had it all become old? The thought of leaving the country one more time and flying alone to some forgotten hole of a place did not appeal anymore. Maybe he was getting old. In any case, it sure wouldn't fit with the lifestyle he planned in the future with Gina.

If he didn't go back to the house...*priorities, man. What is really important?*

He picked up his cellphone—the other cellphone, the one strictly for confidential use—and talked quickly. When done, he put it on the seat beside him and spun the car around. In no time he was on the ramp to the highway speeding back to Langdon Hills.

Becki drove back from the hospital. She felt much better physically, almost euphoric after the stomach episode. But she thought, *I have to get back to the house immediately.*

She considered stopping at the side of the road to phone Karl but decided against it. *Don't waste a minute. Better to get back. Why am I feeling so uneasy? Why in heck am I suddenly so anxious?*

Andrew stood with his hands in his pants pockets and watched the departing car. What a nightmare watching Ian's mom pack up his things. Standing helplessly by, unable to say anything useful. Taking glares from Jerry. As if it was all his fault. As if Ian wasn't always this way, years before Andrew met him.

That was the last time he would see Ian's parents, thank goodness. Oh no, that wasn't right. There was still the funeral. Andrew felt a catch in his throat. He turned back into the motel and hurried down the hall to the room Ian had occupied, making it just in time.

Once in, he pushed the door shut and leaned back on it. Tears were coming now. Hot, steamy tears—the kind that made your eyes sting. He walked over, reached for a tissue on the bedside table and blew his nose.

Oh God, Ian's gone. Happy Ian, clever Ian, fun-loving Ian. Ian, who was like an older brother as well as a lover. Ian, who looked after him.

What was he going to do now?

He sat on the corner of the bed and let the tears come.

"Have you seen Gina?" Anna asked.

Linda stepped out of the BMW and looked at her sister-in-law with disinterest. Nothing much could catch her attention now. Ian was gone. His beautiful belongings were packed neatly into the trunk of their car. Nothing mattered. There was nothing to keep her here anymore.

"Linda, are you all right?"

Linda focused on Anna and took a breath. "No. I haven't seen anyone." She stared into space. *Why won't Anna go away?*

Jerry had walked around the side of the car and was talking with his sister now. What were they saying? Linda could hardly make it out.

"...packing up Ian's belongings...not herself...haven't seen her, but she's with Tony, I think."

Linda stared at the back seat through the window. Ian's argyle sweater sat there, left behind from another journey. She remembered that trip—shopping on Bloor Street in Toronto and then a quick lunch in Yorkville. They had had such fun watching everyone around them...Ian making such caustic, witty remarks about the other patrons. Linda gazed at the pullover lovingly and big tears started to roll slowly down her face.

Reggie sat in the neighbour's cabin cruiser looking through the starboard porthole. Good thing Mark had left him the key in case he felt like fishing. They'd done a lot of fishing together years ago. Mark was a good guy, even if he did allow that shrew of a wife to boss him around.

But now his thoughts focused on the action at the cottage next door. How the hell did the cops find him? What were they doing crawling all over his cottage? He still thought of it as his cottage even though it belonged to his first wife, and they'd been divorced for years.

He leaned back on the blue cushions of the V berth, out of sight. By now the cops would surely know he had been living there. His clothes were scattered about and the laptop—yes, it would be obvious. What would they do next? Send out a search? Luckily he had his wallet with him and a cellphone. The car was still in the driveway, though, and that was a bad sign. They would figure he hadn't gone far.

To be honest, he was surprised. He hadn't thought Carla would go through with charging him. *Damned bitch.* That's what it had to be—unless they still thought he had something to do with Hilary's murder. But surely, they'd figured that one out...or were they too stupid to be real?

He took a chance and glanced out the window. One young guy was down on the dock next door looking about. Reggie knew he couldn't be seen from outside with the sun shining brightly like this. The inside of the boat would appear pitch black. But any time now, one of them might come snooping. Of course, they didn't have a key to get in. Reggie walked quietly over to check the lock again to make sure it was secure. At least there would be a delay as they tried to contact the owners. He slipped silently back to the V berth and peered out the porthole again.

In the dark of the cabin, Reggie frowned. Not only charging him with assault, the damned bitch was setting him up for Hilary's murder. That had to be it. Of all the—

Reggie swore. Sit tight, that's what he had to do for now. Sit tight and think.

The call startled both of them.

Gina's hand went to the portable hall phone. She picked it up and pressed *Talk*.

"Gina speaking," she said automatically. Now why did she say that, like she was at the studio?

"Oh, good. Gina, it's Reggie."

She nearly dropped the phone on the floor. It took everything in her to speak normally into the mouthpiece.

"Hi, how are you?"

"Gina, listen to me. Carla killed Hilary. She's trying to frame me. Are you listening? Are you there…? Gina…say something."

Gina forced her face to go blank. She paused a moment and then said clearly, "Where are you? Are you coming home soon?"

"What is it? Is she there in front of you?"

Gina nodded then realized Reggie couldn't see that. "Yes," she said carefully. "I miss you too, Tony."

"Gotcha," Reggie said. She could hear his sharp intake of breath over the phone. "You're trying to make her think I'm someone else. Get away from her, Gina. Tell Dumont. Oh shit, they're coming. I've got to go now."

The phone clicked. Gina looked up, finding Carla three feet away and staring right at her.

"That wasn't Tony," Carla said. "Who was it?"

Chapter 38

Because Nellie got bored waiting for Gina to come back and play with her, she'd left her room and drifted downstairs. Coming down, she'd noticed through the front door's thick, wavy glass it was snowing again. *Enough to make a fort?*

Maybe. At the bottom of the staircase, she made a fast left to check what it looked like outside on the ground, from the much, much lower window in the living room. Since no one ever used that room, which was just for company, she was really surprised to see Uncle Jerry sitting on the couch.

She knew it was because he was sad about his son's death that he hunched over on the sofa, head in hands, shaking like he had a fever, and didn't even notice when she came in.

She walked toward him, but didn't get very close. Balancing on one foot, then the other, she whispered, "Uncle Jerry?"

He raised his eyes and they were blurry, but he wiped them with the back of his hand and tried a smile. "Hi, Nellie. How are you today?"

"Fine. But you're really sad, aren't you?"

"Yes."

Maybe he's going to start crying even harder.

"It's nice of you to stop and talk to me," he said.

"I know it's hard when someone dies—"

He grabbed hold of the edge of the sofa cushion.

"—because of Grandma," she said. "I miss her a lot, and she was your mom too, right? But know what?"

"What?"

"Mom says Grandma and Ian are in a better place now."

"That's what Mom says, eh?"

"Yup. Think she's right?"

"Maybe." His lips trembled like he was going to say something else.

"What?" she asked.

"Many things I should have done differently. So many things...Nellie, what really, truly matters in this world, is appreciating what you've got—the good people in your life. Your immediate family. Not all the working and working to get more stuff, or impressing others with what you've accomplished. My whole life I tried to prove to my mother how successful I was, and in the end it didn't make a difference. It was just this huge waste of time. She wasn't about to love me any more because of it. And poor Ian..."

For a moment, Nellie thought he might not be able to continue. *He needs a hug.* She inched closer.

"...my poor Ian worked so hard. Took so many punches in his quest to make it to the top. And in the end, do you think he knew how proud I was of him? How much I loved him? No...I don't think so. I was no better than Mother...harsh...critical. And now I have to plan my only son's funeral. Ian's...funeral."

"You and Aunt Linda," Nellie said.

"Me and Aunt Linda..." Then he shook his head like cartoons do when they change their minds. "Here I am burdening you," he murmured, waving her away. "It's not right. You go off now, Nellie. Off to play."

She wanted to do exactly what he said. Run away and forget all about him, and how sad he was. But something made her sidle up and put her skinny arm around his great, shaking shoulders. "You wanna go outside and build a snow fort with me?"

"Of course it was Tony," Gina said. "But he had to hang up. Just like him. His business is always interfering."

Carla realised Gina was trying hard for a hurt expression, but what came across was guilt. "You little brat. Don't you lie to me!" She grabbed her niece by the arm.

Gina yanked it away. "What's with you, Carla? For crying out loud!" She started down the hall. "I'll check on Nellie. I think I've been gone long enough."

"You said Nellie's fine."

"Then I'll let her know you're home, and I'll go on with my

business." In ten paces they reached Nellie's room, and they both saw through the open door Nellie wasn't there. Gina's hand flew to her chest. "Where is she?"

"No need to panic just because she's not in her room. My girl's got the run of the house," Carla said.

"You don't worry about her?" Gina started down the stairs.

Carla followed close behind. "Of course I worry about her. But she can go downstairs by herself without falling. She can make herself a snack in the kitchen. I'm her mother, I know what she is and isn't capable of."

"Does Nellie know what *you're* capable of?" Gina asked under her breath.

Carla caught the tone in the slipstream behind Gina's descending body. And she wanted to explode with pent-up rage. *Little Ms. Perfect. Ms. Cushy Job. Ms. Designer Clothes. Who the hell does she think she is? She doesn't even have kids of her own, and yet pretends to know what's best?*

When the two of them reached the bottom, Carla heard Nellie's voice and said, "My daughter's in there," pointing toward the living room doorway. She peeked inside. "She's fine. She's talking to Jerry."

"Good," Gina said. She pivoted and headed in the direction of the kitchen.

"You didn't answer my question." Carla pursued her as best she could on her stupid cast. "Who was that on the phone?"

"Carla, leave me alone. I want to make myself a cup of tea. And I don't have to answer to you." Once in the back room, she pulled open the door of the cupboard holding the tin of tea bags.

"Do if I say you do."

"Nonsense. You sound like your husband, trying to boss me around."

"Well...I'm tired of being the pushover."

"Is that how you explain it?"

"How I explain what?"

"The way you've been lately."

"What do you mean?"

"Weird—that's all."

"Oh and how would you be if the man you were with, say Tony, beat *you* up, and it was Tony the police were looking for in connection with two murders, and at the same time you had to protect his child?"

Gina whirled. "Reggie says *you* killed Hilary and are trying to frame *him* for it."

Oh boy! The man was going to say she wasn't in bed when he came back from meeting Hilary that night. She'd told him she was checking on Nellie, and he seemed to believe her. But after discovering Hilary had been killed, he raised the issue again and nearly beat the life out of her. And now, apparently, he was outright accusing her. Further complicated by the fact Rob was suspicious of her, and Gina was questioning her about Mom. Now all she needed was for someone to link her to—

"Oh, God. He's right, isn't he?" Gina stared at her, wide-eyed. "The way you looked out the door just now—"

"You're crazy!" Carla hissed.

"Your expression was—"

"Stop it!"

"You killed Grandma first then Hilary."

Carla's blood vessels swelled. Exactly like when Mother got on her case. Like when Mother left her out of her will. Like when Reggie punched her. Like when she watched Reggie and Hilary. Like when Ian taunted her about Hilary.

Enough! She needed to get *control*.

Chapter 39

Rob heard the story second-hand when he got to the precinct. His boss was full of it.

"Waste of time dealing with the locals. Bloody lazy bastards—they couldn't find a hooker at a sales convention, let alone one six-foot male in a three-room cottage." The big man was always good for off-colour metaphors. Rob grimaced, but kept quiet.

"Williamson has been there, all right, even if the locals couldn't find him. He couldn't have gone far, either, with the car right there and the keys on the counter. Probably out fishing somewhere. And with all those idiots crawling around the place like ants on a sandwich, someone probably tipped him off."

McQuarrie stopped to take a breath. His face was red and his blood pressure was zooming—not a good sign. Rob opened his mouth to say something when a country and western song came out of nowhere.

He grabbed for his cellphone.

Carla stopped mid-action. She took a deep breath and called on all her willpower. Then she pushed the knife drawer back in slowly, keeping her back to Gina.

This wasn't the way to do it. Especially not with Gina. No, there had to be another way to get Gina away from here, to stall her so she couldn't tell the others what she'd heard.

"Carla?" Gina's voice behind her was breathless.

Carla leaned on the counter. "Yeah. I'm thinking." It was the truth.

Carla thought quickly. Rob was due to check in. Everyone would be back soon. Becki would be on her way home from the hospital, and who knew when the others would trickle in? She had to get Gina out of here. But how?

Her brows furrowed as her brain calculated. *This is when it helps to be very, very clever,* thought Carla. *Know your prospect. Know what motivates him or her.* And she knew Gina very well.

Carla turned and managed to shudder. "Gina, you can't know what I've been through. Reggie is a manipulative bastard. You know what he's like. I believed all his lies at first, but I don't anymore. You shouldn't, either. Fact is," she said, lowering her voice to almost a whisper, "I'm in danger. Big danger. He nearly killed me once, and he won't stop until I'm dead."

Carla watched as Gina's eyes went wide. *Yes, it's working.*

"I've got to hide. And I need your help."

Gina nodded briefly.

Carla explained what she needed done.

"Dumont," he said into the cellphone.

"What?" It was Reggie's voice on the other end of the phone. Rob was so shocked he nearly fell over. But this was a different Reggie, a flustered son-of-a-bitch who was talking fast and not making much sense. "Where are you?"

Nothing back. Evading, as usual. But—holy crap—what was that he just said about Carla?

"Whoa. Take it again from the top, and tell me everything real slow."

"I wonder what Carla said," muttered Becki as she pulled into the driveway.

So do I.

"Mom!"

Yup, me again.

"Is there some sort of reason why you pop up when you do?" she asked and switched off the engine.

Just that whenever I hear you talking to yourself, I think I might as well provide you with an actual conversation partner.

"Trouble is, and don't take offence—"

I certainly won't.

"—you're not *actual.*"

I can still contribute.

"Can you tell me what's going to happen at the house?"
No.
"Can you assure me things will be fine?"
No.

Becki pushed open the car door with a huff and held it ajar. She noticed she didn't have the strength she used to at her service. Rising from the deep seat with a groan, she mumbled a furtive, "Thanks a lot, Mom." She slammed the door shut and hurried up the walkway.

Tony careened the Audi into the driveway and stood on the brake. He leapt out of the car. Becki appeared in the doorway of the old house.

"Becki, is—"

"She's not here," Becki yelled. She was running gingerly down the steps now. "Jerry says she got into Carla's car just a few minutes ago, and they drove off somewhere."

"Damn." Tony nearly stamped the ground. He frowned and started back to his car. "It's okay. I can follow her. Get in."

Becki reached for the passenger door. The car was already revving.

"Do you know where she'll take Gina?"

"No, but I put a tracer in Gina's purse. As long as she's got her purse." He backed out of the driveway like a demon.

Becki struggled to get her seatbelt done up. "I tried calling her cell, but there's no answer."

"She lost it."

"Tony, I'm scared."

"Me too," he muttered. The car screeched as it coursed onto the main street.

It was all too easy to get Gina out of the house and into the car. Gina had simply stopped for her jacket and purse and followed her out.

"Where are we going?" Gina asked. There was an edge of fear to her voice.

Carla manoeuvred onto the highway and pressed the pedal to the floor. Traffic was light at this time of day, and she easily weaved around slower vehicles to keep her speed up.

"A cabin I know not far from here. The Brownies use it for weekend camps. I was there with Nellie in the summer, and they don't lock it. Reggie doesn't know about it. Nobody does. He'll never find me there."

"But Carla, what will you do? You can't stay there forever."

Carla was driving much too fast. Reckless, she knew. She'd never drive this fast with Nellie in the car. "Just until they find and arrest

Reggie. Then I'll be safe. You can bring me in supplies."

She finished the speech with satisfaction, almost triumph. What a good story, well delivered. She'd always been a great actress. Lots of practice, all these years, hiding the fear and pain. And no one knew. Everyone saw the pretty face, the careful façade of a devoted wife and mother.

"We can stop on the way and pick up stuff."

"No! I have to get there first. Then you can take the car and go back for supplies."

A pause.

Carla risked a glance at Gina, who was frowning.

"What about Nellie?" Gina said.

Carla felt panic for the first time. She'd have to go back to the house for Nellie. After she dealt with Gina. And then they would go away somewhere. But where?

"I don't know." Her mouth was dry. "I don't know what to do about Nellie."

Chapter 40

The parking lot of the camp looked like a frozen snow-covered lake in the middle of the woods. Which it was—in the middle of the woods. It had taken them at least three quarters of an hour to get here from town, even driving at top speed. Now, Gina knew the city—she worked in downtown Toronto with its hustle-bustle in and out of office towers; its horns, sirens and palpable subway rumbles; its colourful store windows and sidewalks crisscrossed with light and shadow; even its hotdog cart aromas and gutter stenches. She was also fondly familiar with small town life, such as in Langdon Hills. But she was unfamiliar with country—rolling farm or wooded cottage—like here. That must be why she felt uneasy. Surely there was nothing menacing about this particular place.

She tried to picture the same scene filled with excited little girls running around in their chocolate brown outfits with little scarves at their necks, but it was hard to imagine because of the two-inch layer of pristine white stuff, broken only by branches that must have snapped and fallen with the weight of early, heavy snow. Her imaging also failed because she suspected Brownies didn't actually wear brown anymore. It was pink they donned now, wasn't it? Or was that the Sparks, the even younger girls?

What am I thinking? Who the hell cares?

"Carla," she said nervously as the car pulled to a stop. "You're absolutely going to freeze here. What's the rush anyway? Surely you could have packed some warm clothes."

"There's a wood-burning fireplace in the main building, so even if they've shut down the electricity for winter, I'll be okay. Come on, let's go see," she said, and hopped out of the car.

Gina followed. The heat and pressure of the sole of Carla's one black leather boot melted the snow she trampled unevenly into a slushy, semi-transparent footprint, beneath which Gina could see an underlying layer of leaves. *Way too cold to be cabin camping!*

In the back of her mind, she knew some crazy enthusiasts slept in thermal sleeping bags, in igloo-like tents, even in the middle of winter, but again too hard to imagine.

Luckily, in one sense Carla was right, and the door of the main lodge squeaked open with one solid push. The entire structure, outside and in, was constructed of wood—whole logs, planks...

Pee-eew. Did the space ever smell dank. Like some hideous, ventless, locker room.

"Okay," Carla said, taking stock, "the kitchen's over there and the supply closet. Would you check the cupboards and see what's available? Hopefully staples like flour, sugar—"

"Not going to be baking brownies," said Gina. *Completely inappropriate humour...*

Carla didn't crack a smile.

Chalk it up to nerves—both the dumb joke and the subsequent non-reaction to the dumb joke.

"Find blankets somewhere," Carla said in her I-mean-business tone. "I'll go back outside and look for firewood. I think there's a woodshed out back."

"Okay, okay..." Gina said, her mood caving. She headed toward the camp kitchen area, which boasted battered pots dangling from the ceiling and an amazing variety of cooking utensils hooked on pegboard. But the more she thought about it, the more she decided this was a stupid, stupid idea and wondered how she ever let herself be convinced to go along with it. Carla would be safe at home if she just told Rob what she'd told her. Reggie was lying. And she was afraid for her life.

It was exactly like when you're confronted by an obnoxious critic, and when you're a TV weather reporter, there are a ton of critics. You can't think of that pulpy reply until it's too late. She saw how they should have handled this situation rather than come all the way out here. It was simple—until the cops had Reggie in custody request the police put a man on guard duty, night and day, outside the house. To prevent anyone from sneaking in. Then Carla and everybody else would be safe.

"Carla," she said, "This is dumb." She turned around. "Listen—"

But Carla was gone.

Oh well, the search for firewood wouldn't take long. Maybe it would even prove unproductive. And in that case, Carla wouldn't...couldn't stay here.

All of a sudden, she heard the sound of a car. Weird, because Carla's was the only vehicle in the lot. She concentrated on listening. There was no doubt about it, a car was moving in the parking lot, breaking the silence of the place with the sound of its motor, the spin of its wheels, and what she interpreted to be the snap of branches under its massive weight. Was Carla using the car to transport wood from an outbuilding to the main building? Or was someone else arriving? That wouldn't be good, would it? She scooted over to the window facing the parking lot and the road. The ledge was festooned with dead flies. She peered out.

"Christ almighty!"

It was Carla. She was high-tailing it down the road away from camp.

Gina almost never swore—always the professional—because you never knew who might overhear, and that would reflect badly on the network. But this time she yelled, "Shit! Shit! Double shit! Triple shit!"

She flew to the door.

What good did it do? Carla was gone, her car no longer visible through the spindly trunks lining the road. And Gina was now stuck in this Godforsaken place. Man, she felt so stupid. Gullible to the nth degree.

She'd been right that moment, when she was standing in the kitchen with Carla, and had that gut feeling Carla was the scary murderer everyone had to be afraid of. *Who was it that said listen to your instincts? 'Cause that's what instincts are for, damn it! To warn you.*

She slammed the door shut and flopped down on the plank floor. She knew she had to strategize her way out of here, but she couldn't think straight. Not through the barrage of thoughts coming from all directions. But. She. Would. Not. Cry.

Civilized society wears down your natural instincts, she realized. *By forcing you to be polite...and politically correct...and considerate...and a good girl...you deny your basic intuitions. After all, you're safe in a civilized society. A society with laws—rules by which everyone is supposed to live.*

But—oh my God!—Carla isn't playing by the rules.

Gina wondered what Tony would think about her massive blunder. On the one side, there he was, not just an architect, but some sort of espionage pro. And here she was, not just a weather babe, but an unbelievable dope. Much more important, she realized, were the lives she'd jeopardised by playing her cards so badly. Could she live with herself if someone else got hurt?

Nellie! Carla might be heading back right now to take Nellie.

Now Gina really felt like crying. What would Dad say?

She imagined him looking up from one of his treasured books as she walked in the room.

"Dad?"

"Yes, dear?" *He'd remove his glasses.*

"I messed up. Did a really stupid thing. And I'm ashamed."

"What in heaven's name do you have to be ashamed of?"

"I had Carla dead to rights, Dad. And I let her go. Actually, she tricked me. And that's what bugs me most. It's ridiculous how naïve I am. Now she's free to hurt more people. And it's all my fault."

"Dearest, come here," *he'd say.*

She'd walk willingly into his arms.

Looking at her with the wisest eyes in the universe, he'd say, "Naïve is not a word for you. You want to believe the best of people, which is a quality, not a sin. If you were guarded or judgemental, you'd be less generous, less loving. You're perfect just the way you are. And I do love you so."

She could almost feel his arms around her. Okay, with his imagined encouragement, she decided she wasn't the only person to give the benefit of the doubt undeservedly. She even went so far as to permit herself to speculate on how many people out there would also give a pass to a woman, especially a blood relation, who was abused by her husband. *But being a victim of abuse doesn't automatically make you...not a murderer.*

No doubt about it, because she didn't have her cellphone, she had to find another means of communication. Likely there'd be no hook-up here, but she'd check it out anyway.

She paced the perimeter of the building, covered every wall and table surface with her eyes. Then she scanned every cubby hole and every storage closet, just in case. No luck. *The outbuildings.*

She left her purse behind because it would only encumber her search, and headed outside to scurry through the dorms and sheds. Nothing. And it was no wonder. Camp leaders would have cellphones with them at all times. And what would be the point in paying for a landline that would only be used seasonally?

If it were just her own fate at stake, she'd go back inside the main lodge now. And wait. And think. But there was sweet Nellie, who was cursed to have the mother from hell, not to mention all the others at home, who didn't know who Carla really was, to consider. She wouldn't let herself think it was too late.

Although they hadn't passed any houses during the last several kilometres of their ride to camp, this area wasn't the great white tundra or anything. She stood in one spot in the middle of the now-muddied tract of snow that was the parking lot and turned around slowly, scanning the horizon.

Evergreen trees. Deciduous trees. Bushes…

Finally, she spotted the top of a silo. *Ah-ha!* There'd have to be a barn attached and a farmhouse nearby, right?

She silenced her cautionary voice. *Yes, I know all about weather.*

Once the daytime high peaked in mid-afternoon, temperature tended to drop. Swiftly. She knew about hypothermia—how cleverly it killed. She supposed Carla counted on it.

But she set out in the direction of the silo anyway.

Chapter 41

Nellie sat on the floor of her bedroom playing with the pink phone. It was real pretty. It even sparkled if you put it in the sunlight.

She'd been hiding it for a few days. Gina had lots of pretty things, but this one—this phone—was special. It was grown-up. Gina talked to Tony on it all the time and everyone knew that Gina and Tony were going steady, just like Barbie and Ken. So Nellie had wanted that phone—wanted to pretend to be going steady and be all grown up too. Besides, it was pink.

Nellie didn't steal things. That was bad. She'd give it back to Gina, so it wasn't stealing. Mom always said you had to share things. Gina would let her share. But even still, she wouldn't tell anyone about it quite yet. Except maybe Macho.

She sat on the floor and pushed numbers with her fingers. Nothing happened. Maybe it needed new batteries like some of her toys did. She pushed a whole bunch of buttons, and then put the phone to her ear as she'd seen Gina do.

"Mr. Policeman?" she said into the phone. "It's me, Nellie. I forgot to tell you something I saw. Something important."

Nellie didn't see Aunt Mandy stop in the hallway. She didn't see her until Mandy came up behind her and said, "Nellie, what are you talking about? What did you see?"

The cellphone in his pocket buzzed insistently. Tony took one hand from the wheel, reached into his pocket.

"You're not supposed to use a cellphone while driving." Becki's words sounded ridiculous, even to herself. Why was she worried about breaking a stupid new law when Gina was in such terrible danger and Tony was already driving at least thirty kilometres over the speed limit on snow?

Tony glanced over at her briefly. The ghost of a smile flickered across his face.

"You talk then."

Becki took the phone nervously, pushed a button—the wrong one—pushed another, and said, "Hello?"

"It's Rob." She turned back to Tony.

Tony swung the Audi onto the shoulder. Snow went flying and for a brief moment, Becki thought they would careen down the bank.

"Give me the phone." Tony's voice was harsh.

"Yeah," he said. "He said what?" Tony turned to Becki. "Reggie says that Carla killed that Best woman. Saw her do it."

Becki felt her mouth go dry. Could it be true? Something deep inside her had flashed a warning...

Carla was not *right*. She was not the person she pretended to be with such enthusiasm. Something dark lurked beneath the exterior.

Becki closed her eyes and tried to concentrate. Carla had killed that poor woman with a baseball bat. And that meant Carla had killed Ian—shot him in cold blood with a gun. It was unthinkable. She couldn't believe it. No, it couldn't be true.

Tony was talking now, giving instructions. "—on the 19th Sideroad, going west, about 17 kilometres from the main highway—"

Why hadn't she told anyone her suspicions? Why hadn't she said something way back? *Mother,* she pleaded, *come now and tell me what to do. Tell me everything is going to be all right.*

"Here, take the phone, and tell him every turn I make."

She blinked at Tony.

"For crissake, Becki, snap out of it."

Becki took the cellphone and forced herself to pay attention.

Jerry sat staring into space. The living room seemed lonely, empty now that Nellie had left to play, and the girls had gone out in the car. Shopping probably. Women could shop anytime, for any reason, it seemed. God knows why they thought it was such an accomplishment, even a triumph, finding *the perfect dress*. How hard can it be spending money someone else earns?

He got up from the desk and went to the bookshelf. So many

volumes here, hardly ever read. That's what he'd always planned to do in his retirement—read the entire room full of books. Escape from his dreary life and have adventures through the pages. That's what Linda didn't understand about books. They weren't boring at all. You could throw yourself in the character's skin and lead another life, if only for a while.

Don't think about Linda lying comatose-like upstairs.

Don't think about Ian. Don't think about the dear misguided boy and the life he could have had.

If only Ian had been a normal boy. If only he had wanted to play baseball and basketball with his dad instead of wanting to go shopping with Mom. If he had been normal, maybe he wouldn't be dead now. Maybe if Jerry had just insisted more...maybe if—

The phone rang. He picked it up automatically.

"What?" It was Dumont. "Carla isn't here." His voice was dull. "Of course, I'll keep her here if she comes back—" Jerry didn't finish the sentence. Comes back for Nellie? Dumont wasn't making any sense. He was saying that Carla killed that woman. His sister Carla. He wasn't hearing right. Carla killed Ian. Her own nephew. Dumont was still talking, but the phone had fallen from Jerry's hand and it hit the floor with a thud.

"Jerry, what is it?"

Jerry looked blindly at his sister, Anna. Where had she come from? The room had been empty a moment ago.

"Jerry, where is everyone? Where's Gina?"

Jerry stared at her worried face. His mouth felt dry and full of fluff.

Anna went to the study window. "I can't find Becki, and her car's right there. Where is she? And Carla?"

At the name, Jerry shook himself free of stupor. *Good God, Gina has gone out alone with Carla. And Carla is a killer.*

The snow was coming down now in big, sideways flakes. Gina had always hated snow. No matter how pretty it looked, it was still rotten. She was cold now, standing in the middle of the endless flurries, shivering.

She hadn't dressed for snow. She wasn't even dressed for winter because, dammit—it was only October. Who expected snow in October? Only a few days ago, she and Tony were sitting against the old maple watching the leaves fall. Where was Tony now, she wailed to herself. Why the hell did he have to leave her alone to go to his rotten job? She wrapped her thin arms more tightly around the fuchsia wool pea jacket, *a steal at two-fifty, but who the hell cares if you freeze to death in it?*

It had been stupid to walk away from the cabin. Car tracks led to the cabin, and that's where everyone would look for her. *That is, if they were looking for her,* she thought bitterly. Who would guess? Who would even think to finger Carla for the murders?

The silo was quickly disappearing from view. She had started out before the snow had gotten heavy. Now she couldn't tell if the silo was getting closer or not. *How could you even see what direction you were going in now?* But she had to keep walking to get to a phone to warn everyone.

The big question was—what would Carla do now? *Put yourself in Carla's shoes,* she told herself. *Keep walking, but keep thinking too. Don't think of your feet freezing in these useless suede boots. Think of what Carla would do next...what you would do if you were Carla.*

That's easy, Gina thought firmly. *Go back for Nellie.*

Chapter 42

"What did you see, honey?" Aunt Mandy repeated.
Nellie had heard the first time. "Pretending," she said.
"Like you're talking to a policeman?"
"Uh-huh."
"Detective Dumont?"
"Some other policeman."
"Ah…Not fond of Detective Dumont?"
"He's okay."
"Hey, isn't that a real phone?" Aunt Mandy held out a hand for the pink cell.
Nellie handed it over.
"You're allowed to play with it?"
"I'm *borrowing* it."
"Going to give it back when you're done?"
"Yes."
"Good girl." Aunt Mandy handed it back. "I'm heading downstairs for a snack. Your mom lets you have a snack in the afternoon, right? Want to join me?"
"Can I keep playing a bit?" Nellie asked, looking up at Aunt Mandy.
"Sure."
She barely heard Aunt Mandy's footfalls on the stairs going down. Good thing it was Aunt Mandy who stopped by, and not her grown-up

son, Tony. Tony would have asked a whole lot more questions. And he would have known it was Gina's phone. He would have made her give it back right away. He was...strict.

But even Tony wouldn't be able to make her tell. Not pretend tell, but really tell about seeing that dead lady right here in her room. It was okay to lie about some things. Like when you don't want to hurt someone's feelings. Like when you don't want Mom to know how giggly that lady and Father were that night and how it looked like she was Father's girlfriend.

But she told the pretend policeman everything because it made her feel better. Then she pressed a button like she saw Gina do before hanging up. And then—whoa!—she heard Aunt Becki.

"Gina, it's Becki. So...I'm the one who's in hospital now. I know. Dumb. Something I ate. Anyway, I discovered something here. By fluke. My doctor, Dr. Crosby, is...was...Godmom's doctor too. And he happened to let it slip that Godmom didn't have cancer. You believe that? What's it mean, do you think? Was Carla lying? Or was she somehow convinced Godmom had cancer? Weird, huh? So I want to talk to you about it. Call me. Room 27. They're forcing me to stay here overnight. So call anytime. Don't worry how late. Believe me, I'm getting plenty of sleep. And Gina...be careful. Something's seriously not right about this. Okay...bye for now."

Grandma didn't have cancer? Mom lied? And Gina was supposed to be careful because—something was wrong? *Oh, man.* She tossed the pink phone into the corner where it belonged. Her bottom lip pushed out—her sulky face, Mom called it.

Finally, she decided she was going down for her snack. On her way downstairs, she noticed it looked like a bad blizzard outside. She hurried toward the kitchen, where she heard hushed voices. Aunt Mandy was there. She could see her through the doorway. And she recognized Uncle Jerry. She was good with voices.

"We're all who seem to be in the house right now," he was saying. "Except for Linda...I want her to sleep," he said. Then he stopped.

"Out with it," Uncle Gord said.

"Spit it out, bro."

That was Aunt Anna's voice. A family meeting or something? Nellie decided not to barge in. Especially since Uncle Jerry obviously didn't count her as part of the family. So she ducked into the library to listen and not be seen.

"Dumont says it's not Reggie who's the killer, like we've all been thinking, but Carla."

Nellie's body started to shake. She felt like screaming.

"What?" Aunt Anna exclaimed.

Her aunt must be as shocked as Nellie was.

"Come on. We all know if it has to be one of us, it's Reggie. Right?"

"Hmmm," Uncle Gord said. "Maybe not."

"How did Dumont get this brilliant idea?" Aunt Mandy asked.

"From Reggie."

"Get real. And Dumont is listening to *him*?"

"Well, Reggie disclosed where he's been all this time. And he's alibied for...for Ian's murder. A friend of his out Kingston way."

"But still."

"Claims he actually saw Carla kill that Best woman."

Nellie clutched her stomach.

"Ya, right. So after witnessing his wife kill someone, he leaves town? Without telling the cops or anything? Leaves his daughter with—?"

"Could be he thought he killed Carla before he left."

Nellie gagged.

"Talk about nuts. Now it's Reggie's word against hers."

"Bad news is," Uncle Jerry said, "if it's Carla, then Gina might be in danger. Saw them leave together."

"Oh no!" Aunt Anna gasped.

"Our girl will be fine," Uncle Gord said. "Gina's smart. Capable. And maybe Dumont's got it all wrong."

Nellie imagined Uncle Gord getting up from his chair, walking over to his wife and putting his arms around her. She wished for arms around her too. Out of the corner of her eye, she saw movement at the front end of the hall. Cold rushed past her. Mom stepped inside the front door. She had snow stuck all over her. First thing she did when she saw Nellie was hold a pointed finger in front of her lips.

Shhhh.

Since Aunt Mandy was directly in line with the front door, she must have felt the draft, as well. She whirled in her chair. "Carla!"

The sound of chairs scraping against tiles. Everyone shouting at once. The gang in the kitchen funnelling out and accusing Mom. Mom yelling back at them. Mom signalling Nellie with her finger. This time it meant *Come here*. Of course, she wanted to be with Mom more than anyone else. But Mom was ever in a mood. Nellie guessed it was because she stumbled—hesitated. Both Aunt Mandy and Aunt Anna were insisting she not go to Mom. Maybe she should just run and hide for a while. What to believe? Who to believe? Not Father. Mom? Mom called them white lies. Maybe Mom lied about Grandma. But why did everyone think she could kill someone? Mom had a smile on her face.

Well, it *looked* like a smile.

Before Nellie could move an inch, a hulking figure appeared in the doorway behind Mom. Detective Dumont. He pulled her hands behind her, snapped on handcuffs. "You're under arrest."

"Mommy!" Nellie sobbed.

Racing down the hall, she wrapped her arms around Mom and pressed her face against Mom's stomach. *Mommy...*

Chapter 43

"Everything's going to be fine, honey," Carla said, wishing she could put her hands on her child's head, run her fingers through her soft, but matted hair, cup her tiny chin, and lift her face so Nellie could see the truth in her one and only caring parent's eyes. "See, honey, darling, grown-ups make mistakes. I know, I know…" she comforted. Poor Nellie was bawling harder than she'd ever witnessed. "Great, big, huge mistakes even," she continued. "Like Detective Dumont. He's making a whopper." She said this partly for the benefit of the others, who'd gathered around her like a posse. "And he'll correct it soon enough." Before crouching down on a level with Nellie, she twisted around, and bore holes through Rob Dumont with her eyes.

"We'll see about that. Where's *my* daughter? Where's Gina?" Anna demanded.

Normally big sister Anna was a poster woman for poise. Now she looked like *she* required restraints. And Carla had never seen brother-in-law Gord look menacing before. Rob had to hold him off with his hand.

The world turned upside-down. How could they stand by while Rob arrested her? How could they think she'd allow herself to harm someone? Gina? Pent-up emotion threatened to erupt inside her, but she forced herself calm. Wasn't she expert at tamping down? Reggie put her through her paces over and over again through the years, didn't he? And basically, when you came right down to it, once again it was Reggie who laid this shit on her. *Bastard! And to think I tried to warn him.*

Mostly she tried to think like Nellie's mother. And remember her sister was a mother too. Worried about her child.

"Gina's fine, Anna. She's safe. I left her at a Brownie camp outside town—"

"What'd you do that for?" her brother-in-law demanded.

"Trying to avoid this very situation," she started to explain.

"Trying to avoid getting caught," Rob said.

"Yes, but—"

"You killed my son. You freaking killed my son!" Jerry looked like a heart attack waiting to happen.

"Let me finish. I *was* trying to avoid getting caught, just like Rob said."

She was interrupted again by screeches from the posse. Nellie clamped onto her so tightly, Carla found it hard to breathe.

"What I mean is I was trying to avoid getting caught in Reggie's lies. See? He's trying to squirm out of serving time for beating me up." She looked around and wondered if she seemed like someone pleading for her life, which is just what she felt like. "That's exactly what he's trying to do." *Unless he really believes I did it.*

"He thinks if he sets me up as the murderer, as a monster, the case against him will be dropped. But—reality check—I'm no murderer. He's conning you. Tell me you see it!" How depressing to have her own family, not to mention the long arm of the law, believe her abusive husband over her.

"Maybe not," she said, watching them, and then she heaved a sigh. "'Cause Reggie's a pro. He's been lying and manipulating and getting away with it for years. He's convincing all right. And because the tension's so high around here, with these murders right outside our door, we're all secretly wondering about each other. Aren't we? Doubting. Even Gina."

No one budged.

"Hard to believe." she said. "Once the deadly virus of suspicion breaks out..." She shrugged. "I'll admit I was scared. Especially when I found out Reggie was accusing me. And on top of that, Gina—of all people—let me know she suspected me, as well. I thought I was done for. And my God, my daughter needs me. So what did I do? I tried to buy time. Until the *real* murderer gets caught. Until things sort themselves out. But now here I am." She rattled her cuffs behind her back. "Am I getting through to you at all?"

She felt herself running out of strength. But she had to make them see. "You've known me all my life, Jerry, Anna. We may not be close or anything, but for God's sake, you know I'd never kill anyone."

"Prove it," Gord said. "Take us to Gina."

"Now," Anna said.

Carla knew Anna would show her no compassion until she saw Gina with her own two eyes. "I will. Rob?"

He nodded. "Beside me in my cruiser. Lead the way, Carla. The rest of you can follow."

"What about Nellie?" Carla asked.

"She can come with us," Mandy offered.

"Fine." She whispered in her daughter's ear, "Go with Aunt Mandy." If only her hands were free. But she could only soothe and coax. "Everything will be fine. I promise. I'm going to take us to Gina. You'll see. Go with Aunt Mandy now. Okay, hon? Please."

Nellie swiped at her tears, turned, then raised her voice and stated very clearly for all to hear, "My mother would never hurt a fly. And you should all know that." Then she stalked over to her aunt.

"Carla, are you saying it's Reggie, then?" Jerry asked. "'Cause if it is, I'll kill him."

Carla sighed. *There they go again, jumping to conclusions.* "It's not Reggie, Jerry. If I thought it was him, I'd have turned him in myself. The—" She stopped herself. "He's only a threat to me. Not to his daughter. And not to anyone else, either. Although, if he doesn't smarten up, I can see him headed in that direction."

"What makes you so sure it's *not* him?" Rob asked.

"Because I saw him that night. Meeting Hilary."

Jaws dropped.

"I followed him. I knew he had a meeting with someone. I thought it was because he was gambling again. Thought maybe he had a debt to pay off or something. Believe me, it didn't warm my heart to catch him with another woman."

She shifted. The cuffs stretched her arms behind her back. "It looked like they were arguing behind the garage. Didn't get close enough to hear what they said. Don't care anyway. Thing is, when he left her, she was intact. So Reggie didn't kill her. And I—"

"Yes, you," said Rob. His voice still carried a dose of mistrust.

"I scrambled back to our bedroom. Got there shortly after Reggie."

"Why should we believe you?" Anna asked.

"Why would Carla protect that misfit of a husband of hers?" Gord put in. "After he's accused her."

"Well, if it's not Carla, and it's not Reggie, who the hell did it?" asked a voice that floated from the top of the stairs. Linda looked unsteady, like she might come tumbling down the staircase. "Who killed my son?"

Tony barrelled down the lane. He sped the vehicle up as they approached their final destination, as proved by the sign further back that read *Dead End*. Nowhere else to go except straight ahead to the Girl Guides of Canada summer camp. Although he noted fewer details than he normally would, he did notice Becki clutching the passenger door.

Rob had hung up on them earlier. *I'll call you right back,* he'd said. Then nothing. Normally, Tony would have tried to make conversation, but not now, because Gina—Gina was all that mattered.

His phone rang. Becki picked up immediately. "Hello?" She made a rolling motion with her other hand. "Keep going, Tony. I'll tell you everything he says."

They hit something hidden under the snow. Even with its excellent shocks, the Audi bounced them so that Tony banged his head on the roof. "Christ!"

"Rob says Carla's at home—ha!—in handcuffs."

"Gina?" Tony broke in.

"Where's Gina?" Becki asked.

The windshield wipers furiously beat off snow.

"Not with her."

It made sense. Tony's tracer indicated she was near. Now he could see a break in the canopy of trees. The sun's last effort flooded the open area. Oh, God. What would he find?

"Carla says she left Gina at the camp. She says Gina's fine."

To Rob on the phone, Becki said, "Do we believe her? Is Gina—"

"She'd better be fine." Tony cursed. "Tell Rob that."

Becki didn't follow orders well. Instead, she turned to Tony. "He says they're on their way here."

Tony skidded to a stop in the parking lot, shot out of the car. Even if he wasn't gathering clues, they popped out at him from under the snow and slush of the parking lot. Tire tracks. Nearly obliterated by snowfall. One vehicle. It had come and gone in a spray of mud.

Footprints led up to the main building ahead. Two sets. Gina's. And Carla's, her cast making an over-sized impression. Further print trails spread out from the log cabin.

His architectural expertise abandoned, Tony was straight cop now. Or not. Gina was inside. Tracer told him.

He threw open the door. "Gina!"

No answer.

"Gina!" Becki called with him.

Their voices rang through the empty space.

Tony looked everywhere.

"Tony," Becki said.

He whirled around to face her. "What?"

"Her purse." She pointed.

There it sat, abandoned on one of the wood tables in the middle of the room.

"She's not here," he said, his heart thundering in his ears.

Chapter 44

Gina saw them—Tony and Becki—coming through the snow. They were nearly here, nearly to her. *Oh, thank God.* They lifted her, hugged her, kissed her. The warmth, the glorious warmth. She could fold herself into it, lose herself in it. But she had something to do first.

"Thank God," she mumbled. "Give me your cellphone."

"What did she say?" Tony asked Becki.

"Something about a cellphone. Gina, darling, you don't need it now. We're here."

"Give it to me." Gina grabbed on to Becki's sleeve. "Please."

"She must be dazed by the cold."

"I'm not dazed, Becki. You don't understand. I know who—"

Tony huffed. "Give her the damned cellphone, Becki."

Gina grabbed it and tried to turn it on, but her fingers wouldn't work. She nearly screamed in frustration. She shoved it back at Becki. "You dial. I can't."

Becki stared at her, but started pushing the numbers that Gina recited.

As soon as she was done, Gina grabbed the phone. In a flash, her face transformed and her voice became silk. "Tina, darling. It's Gina. Yes, I'm still up here, and it's freezing cold. Look, I'm in a hurry—thanks, darling. Now listen…"

She glanced at Tony and rolled her eyes. "Tina, remember poor Hilary Best? We talked about her last week. Well, you know her sister,

Andrea?" Pause. "Uh-huh? What do you know about—she did? She tried to—and they wouldn't? That's what I wanted to know. Look, I'll call you as soon as I'm back in town. Lunch?" Another pause. "Thanks, darling."

She tried to click the phone off, but her thumb wouldn't work. Tony took it gently from her and ended the call. She stood shivering, but there was a big smile on her face.

Tony raised a brow. "What was that all about?"

"I know who the killer is. And it isn't Carla."

The Audi was headed south at a furious pace. The others had been warned to turn around and head back. Gina was coming home.

"It was when I was wandering. I had to think of something to keep myself awake, and I went back over the crime. The first crime. It all comes back to that. What happened? Hilary Best died. Who would want her dead? Carla maybe, if it were true Hilary was having an affair with Reggie. And maybe Reggie, if things had gone sour with the affair. But we missed a whole point. A whole avenue of discussion."

Gina's voice was still a bit shaky, but the confidence was there.

"Who would want Hilary dead? Was there anyone else who could gain from Hilary's death? Was there—for instance—any money at stake? Did someone inherit?"

Gina heard Tony curse. She smiled.

"Actually, a lot of money. Hilary had come through an expensive divorce. She owned a swank condo and a cottage in Muskoka that had to be worth millions. And she had no children or husband or parents left alive. Just a sister." *A sister who hated her,* Gina remembered.

She glanced at Becki, who kept one arm around her, warming her still.

"It's as I thought. Tina says Andrea tried to return several pricey items to Holt's last week. They wouldn't take them back because they were last season and some of the things had the tags missing—obviously worn. Andrea threw a hissy fit and stalked out. I think her husband was part of that development company that just went under. What's the name?"

"Denman's."

"That's it. Andrea needed money fast. I'll bet she was going to bail from the husband before the courts took everything. She probably followed Hilary up here and argued with her."

Becki's voice was rich and comforting. "But would anyone really kill their own sister just for money?"

Tony laughed. "Is there any better reason?"

Gina frowned. Her mind was working efficiently now, pulling out memories. *Andrea? Andrew...the names...so similar.*

"Oh, I think there's something more behind it. I can't be sure, but I heard a rumour once...Something about an unwanted pregnancy, long ago..."

Dumont stared. Killers came in all packages, it was true. But he couldn't believe the cool demeanour of the woman in front of him, the woman who had brutally murdered her own sister.

"So. You inherit."

Andrea blew out smoke. "Probably. I can't be sure, she might still have her ex in the will, but I doubt it. And I don't think she would have put Reggie in yet. So it's probably left to me."

Dumont paused. She said it so calmly, as if it didn't matter.

"You killed her not knowing if you would inherit?" This didn't seem logical to him. Wouldn't you check first?

Andrea snapped her gaze to Dumont. She carefully butted the cigarette on the tin ashtray.

"You think I did this for money?" Her eyes flashed.

Was it anger? Dumont couldn't tell. "Why else?"

Andrea shook her head. "You don't get anything, do you? Just stumbling around trying to find clues and you don't understand the least of what motivates us. I guess we do seem different to you."

Now Dumont was angry. *Enough of the damned class differences.* It made his blood boil, how this woman thought she was better than everyone else...but she was talking again. He better listen.

"It was about Andrew. Don't you get it? I found out Hilary was dating Andrew, was having an *affair* with Andrew. How could she?"

Finally Dumont was getting it. "And you wanted Andrew for yourself?"

Andrea's eyes went wide. "Don't be absurd. It was disgusting. Her own nephew. And she laughed when I told her. Laughed like it was something funny. And I saw the baseball bat, and I had to stop her disgusting laugh. I had to right then and there."

Dumont couldn't quite grasp—

"Don't you get it? Andrew is my son."

Chapter 45

"One more thing I don't understand. How did you even know Ian?"

Rob was perplexed. It was the last piece of the puzzle he couldn't put together. They were at the precinct now, eyeing each other across a dull grey table. Andrea seemed cool, resigned. She had come without a fight…she had merely sighed, looked at Dumont and quipped something about always wanting to try handcuffs.

Now Andrea nodded. "Simple, really. He has this design show on cable—you've seen it?"

Dumont shook his head.

"He's really quite good. Was." She reached for another cigarette, tapping it out of the pack. "I called the studio to get his name. He did over my house two years ago. Very mid-century modern with a Euro edge, you know?"

Dumont didn't.

She flicked the lighter. A flame burst vermilion. She put it to the cigarette and inhaled.

"So you met—"

Andrea looked over. "Soon after we finished the project, I was lunching with Hilary at the Bloor Street Diner, and who walks over but Ian, with Andrew in tow. You could have knocked me over with a feather when Ian introduced us. Of course, I knew who he was. Andrew, that is. I knew the family who adopted him, knew the name. It was all done privately through the doctor I had at the time."

She took a puff and looked off into space.

Could it really be that simple? Dumont felt like cursing.

"Hilary must have snagged Andrew's phone number right then and there. She always was a bloody cow, sniffing after young blood. I didn't find out about it until two weeks ago when I went to the cottage in Muskoka to look for an old photo album Mom had. It really isn't important. And there was Andrew. My Andrew. At our old cottage waiting for Hilary. I could have screamed."

She sniffed and turned back. "He doesn't know he's my son, you see. Nobody knew. So what could I do?"

Dumont could see it all now. Andrea following Hilary to Langdon Hills. Starting a confrontation in the back behind the garage, by the forest, away from prying eyes. Losing her temper...

"I'm sorry about Ian. He saw me leave the parking lot of that crummy motel. He knew Hilary was my sister. He put two and two together and figured I had been there at the scene. And, of course, he knew my phone number. We agreed to meet later for lunch in town so I could explain, but—" She paused.

"You found him on the deck first," Dumont said.

She nodded then frowned. "I don't think he even knew about Andrew. About my connection or about Hilary. I feel bad about Ian. Too bad he was such a cat."

Curiosity killed the cat. Dumont got that one.

"The gun?"

Andrea shrugged. Then she smiled. "You can buy anything in Toronto if you know the right people."

"Karl, I'm coming home right after the funeral," Becki said over the phone. Did her voice convey how excited and relieved she was?

"Great news. Loneliest couple weeks of my life."

"Hey, don't pile it on too thick."

"Huh?"

"I know a man needs time on his own now and again. Doesn't need to be joined at the hip to his wife."

"You telling me our honeymoon phase is over?"

"We could start a new one," she suggested, brightening. "Gina and Tony sure seem headed in that direction. And it looks like a whole lot of fun to me."

"You know how they always talk about the astronomical divorce rate?"

"Oh." Her heart spasmed. Gone too long, after all. "Sure."

"Fifty percent or something like that?"

"Right," she acknowledged. "Bad."

"But the other fifty percent of marriages succeed. And don't need to be resuscitated. That's ours."

Phew. "Sweet! Hope things work out the same for Gina and Tony. You'll be interested to know Gina's a fabulous amateur sleuth. Not to mention the way she looks. And dresses. What happened is I got food poisoning and had it figured wrong."

"That surprises me the way you've been solving mysteries in Black Currant Bay."

"Well, Carla was just trying to protect her family. But Gina? It's like she has a nose for more than just the weather. She must sense a...climate, or something."

"Hmmm. You make a great team."

"I suppose Rob Dumont would have got it eventually. Not a bad guy. Not really. What happened was Gina distracted him."

"What? Threw him off, did she? So she could close the case herself?"

"Don't be ridiculous. It's obvious he has a crush on her, and it probably affected his powers of deduction. But he's got everything wrapped up solid now. Both Andrea and Reggie are in custody."

"And Carla and Nellie?"

"They'll be fine. Carla found her mojo."

"Mojo?"

"That's the word they use, isn't it?"

"Who?"

"Young people."

"You mean young*er* people."

"Not-middle-aged people. The up-and-coming generation. Like Gina and Tony."

"Ahh, the successful couple."

"Well...Rob's still waiting in the wings. Tony better mind his p's and q's."

"It's still hard to believe all this had nothing to do with the will."

Gina sat sipping espresso beside Tony on the comfy mocha sofa in her uptown condo. Throw cushions surrounded her on both sides while light poured in from the floor-to-ceiling windows. It was pure heaven to be back in the city after Ian's funeral and away from the rest of the family. *Much as she loved them. Better add that.*

Tony shrugged. "Not everything is about money. Don't let the husband's court case fool you. These people have money stashed away in all sorts of foreign accounts. Andrea has lots of it, believe me. Not that she'll be able to use it for a long time."

Gina frowned. "So it was all about image? How silly. Who would care that Andrea had an illegitimate baby long ago?"

Tony shook his head. "It wasn't about that. I think it was about Hilary taking something that belonged to Andrea. The son she never got to know. And here was Hilary, stamping her brand on him in an admittedly creepy way. Andrea went a little nuts. And poor Ian got in the way."

She fell into deep thought. *Poor, dear Ian, never quite fitting in. Craving the applause that came with being a television celebrity...always seeking acceptance. They wouldn't forget him. No, they wouldn't.*

And then she had a sudden idea.

"Perhaps we could establish a scholarship in Ian's name."

Tony sat up abruptly. "What an excellent idea, Squirt. We could use the money that should have gone to him. I'll contact the college he went to and see about setting it up."

Gina found she could smile now. It was a fitting memorial. "Ian would like that."

They sat in companionable silence. The condo was tiny, and it seemed full with Tony in it...maybe too full. It really was meant for one person. Maybe she should think about upgrading to a two-bedroom now that she had the money. Maybe—

She sipped again from the nearly empty cup. "It will be strange to have money. I mean, real money. What are you planning to do with yours?"

Tony put his espresso cup down on the glass coffee table and turned to her.

"I've been drawing up plans for a house. Something just outside the city, for the two of us."

Gina blushed. "The two of us?"

"Well, I'm allowing for four. And a dog. But it could always be expanded if you want more than two kids. One thing I've allowed for...it will have plenty of closets."

She laughed. "You'll never stop teasing me about being a fashionista."

"Hell, no," he said. "I still can't get over you beating the cops to the punch with that purse clue. Who would have thought the identity of a victim would spin on the pedigree of her purse?"

"That's the appeal of haute couture," she said. "Things are unique. Like the houses you design."

"Well done," he admitted. "You've deftly turned me into one of you."

Gina turned to face him full-on. It was now or never—the question that would determine both their futures. She had to ask.

"Tony, tell me truthfully. You're really going to be able to leave your other work and settle down as a real architect?"

Tony grinned and reached for her. "I've always been a real architect. And there's nothing more I want than to settle down with you."

~*~

Message from the Authors

Dear Reader,

Here it is—our first Fashionation with Mystery novel. We started this novel as an adventure cooked up over a lunch out. Can two friends—both mystery writers—combine their talents to produce one exciting and romantic mystery novel? Can they do it and still remain friends? Yes!

Writers are a possessive lot. We work meticulously to make our words just perfect. Working with another person means compromising…but it also means delighting in the twists and turns of plot that your partner can surprise you with. Not to mention, the enjoyment of meeting over additional lunches. The experience was so positive we're keeping the ball of yarn rolling, so stay tuned to fashionationwithmystery.com to stay abreast of the latest fashion trend—in mystery.

Yours truly,

Melodie and Cynthia

About Melodie Campbell

Melodie has a Commerce degree from Queen's University, but it didn't take well. She has been a bank manager, marketing director, college instructor, comedy writer and possibly the worst runway model ever.

Melodie got her start writing comedy. In 1999 she opened the Canadian Humour Conference. She has over 200 publications, including 40 short stories and has won 6 awards for short fiction. Her first novel, **Rowena Through the Wall**, is an Amazon bestseller. Melodie was a finalist for the 2012 Derringer Award and Arthur Ellis Award, and is the General Manager of Crime Writers of Canada.

http://www.melodiecampbell.com

About Cynthia St-Pierre

In marketing Cynthia wrote promotional, packaging and communications materials; penned articles for business periodicals; and a chapter of *How to Successfully Do Business in Canada*. Currently a member of Crime Writers of Canada, she has one award for fiction and has been a writing contest judge. Best of all for a mystery writer, Cynthia has received a York Regional Police Citizens Awareness Program certificate, presented and signed by Julian Fantino, former Commissioner of the Ontario Provincial Police.

In addition, Cynthia grows vegetables in her backyard, makes recipes with tofu, and speaks English-accented French with husband Yves. Visit Cynthia's blog (in the voice of character Becki Green) at vegetariandetective.blogspot.com.

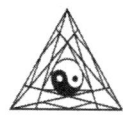

IMAJIN BOOKS
Quality fiction beyond your wildest dreams

For your next ebook or paperback purchase, please visit:

www.imajinbooks.com

www.twitter.com/imajinbooks

Made in the USA
Charleston, SC
22 July 2012